THE BETROTHED

Sisters of Woodside Mysteries
Book 0

A Regency Romance

by Mary Kingswood

Published by Sutors Publishing

Cover design by: Shayne Rutherford of Darkmoon Graphics

About this book: *A traditional Regency romance, drawing room rather than bedroom.*

Rosamund Winterton is ready to settle down. At two and twenty, she determines to bring a previous suitor to the point. When he proposes and she accepts, her future seems assured. But the death of her betrothed just days before the wedding leaves Rosamund desperate for a replacement, and his younger brother seems ideal. There's just one problem — Rosamund can't stand him.

Robin Dalton just wants to carve out a place for himself in London society, and marrying a provincial chit like Rosamund doesn't come into it. Still, she's very pretty and there's a good dowry, so perhaps it won't be so bad. But marriage is surprisingly difficult, and however did he come to fall in love?

But their fragile chance of happiness hangs by a thread; the constables are suspicious about his elder brother's death, and Robin is the obvious suspect. How can he possibly prove his innocence?

A prequel to the 5-book Sisters of Woodside Mysteries series, each a complete story with a HEA, but read all of them to find out all the family secrets!

About the series: *When Mr Edmund Winterton of Woodside dies, his daughters find themselves penniless and homeless. What can they do? Unless they wish to live on charity, they will have to find genteel employment for themselves. This book is set in England during the Regency period of the early nineteenth century. Book 0 takes place 5 years before books 1-4, and book 5 ten years later.*

Book 0: The Betrothed (Rosamund) (a short novel, free to mailing list subscribers)

Book 1: The Governess (Annabelle)

Book 2: The Chaperon (Lucy)

Book 3: The Companion (Margaret)

Book 4: The Seamstress (Fanny)

Book 5: Woodside

Table of Contents

The Winterton family

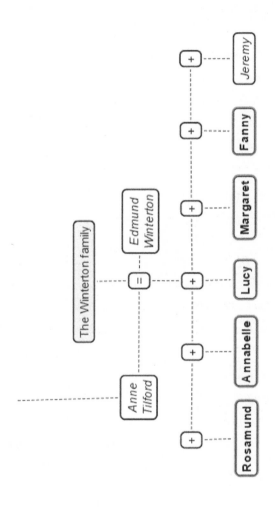

The Dalton family

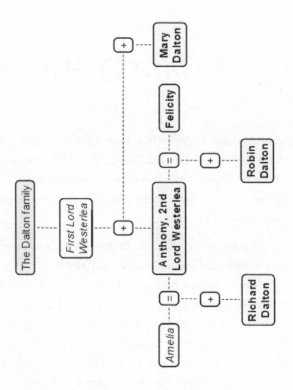

You can obtain high resolution versions of these family trees at my website at http://marykingswood.co.uk/.

1: An Offer Of Marriage

Miss Rosamund Winterton rode round to the Woodside stables in a state of unusual excitement. The news she had to impart was such as must bring pleasure to her sisters, at least. To her father — well, there was no saying how Papa might react.

She slid gracefully from Midnight's back as soon as the groom had hold of the bridle, and strode into the house through the garden door. On any other day she would have taken herself and her mud-spattered habit straight upstairs, but not today. Most likely everyone could be found in the morning room, and a little mud in that part of the house was of no consequence. It was their comfortable working room, their refuge from the polite world of morning calls. Surrounded by the familiar battered old furniture, unchanged for decades, they passed the hours when no other duty called, sewing, reading, practising their music and gossiping together.

All her sisters were there. Annabelle was curled up in a wing chair near the window, reading. Fanny was embroidering a reticule with her nimble fingers. Margaret was pleating a ribbon for a bonnet with intense concentration. And Lucy was chattering, naturally. Lucy was always chattering.

Four heads lifted as one as Rosamund entered the room. Fanny and Lucy smiled at her warmly. Margaret's face was bewildered, her mind still busy with her ribbons. But Annabelle — ah, Annabelle was the clever one of the family, for she threw down her book and jumped up at once, puzzled by Rosamund's appearance in her riding clothes.

"Rosie? What has happened?"

"Richard has asked me to marry him, and I have agreed to it." Then, with a ripple of laughter, she added, "I am going to change, so if you want to know everything, you must come to my room."

They did indeed want to know everything, so they tripped up the stairs behind her in a giggling cluster. Being the oldest Winterton sister, and two and twenty years of age, Rosamund had her own room with a pleasant view over the stables and the park beyond. Her four sisters arrayed themselves on the bed, as Rosamund peeled off her habit and washed away the sweat of her ride.

"Come on, Rosie, tell us the whole story," Lucy cried.

"There is not much to tell," Rosamund said.

"But we want to hear all of it," Lucy said, giggling.

"Oh yes!" said Fanny, her doe eyes wide. "Was it romantic?"

"Not very," Rosamund said, smiling. "Our paths crossed on Rivers Common, he proposed and I said yes."

"Oh," the sisters said in disappointed tones.

"There must be more to it than that," Lucy said. "He has already proposed twice, so what made him try again?"

"And why did you accept him?" Annabelle said gently.

"Are you quite in love with him?" Fanny said.

"In love? Not at all," Rosamund said crisply. "I simply decided that it was time, that is all. This is the third time he has asked, and I could not depend on a fourth time. Now, who will help me into my gown?" Margaret jumped up at once.

"What will Papa say?" Fanny said timidly.

"He can have no objection to Richard Dalton," Annabelle said quickly. "None at all."

"But he will not like you leaving Woodside," Lucy said.

"I dare say Papa will not even notice my absence," Rosamund said.

"Of course he will, for who will order his brandy when you are gone?"

The sisters laughed, but there was no warmth in it, for Lucy's words were all too true.

~~~~~

That afternoon, Rosamund changed into one of her best morning gowns and waited in the drawing room with her tapestry. Around her, her sisters twittered excitedly, but she was calm. It was, after all, what she had chosen for herself.

The question of how to bring on a renewal of Richard's addresses had occupied her thoughts for some time now, so it was pleasant to have the matter settled at last.

Richard arrived, exactly as he had promised, at three o'clock and was shown directly into Papa's book room. Twenty minutes later, Havelock, the housekeeper, came for her.

"Mr Winterton would like you to join him and Mr Dalton in the book room, miss."

"Thank you, Havelock."

She walked behind the housekeeper without haste. For the first time, a tremor of fear fluttered in her stomach. Papa could not prevent her marrying Richard, but there was still the question of a dowry, which had never been made clear, no matter how many times she had asked. There was nothing settled, so it was for Papa to determine how much each of the sisters would have, when the time came for them to marry.

Havelock opened the door for her and she entered her father's book room, very much his sanctuary since Mama had died. Here he sat, day after day, pretending to read, a bottle of brandy always on the table beside him. It was a dark, masculine room, with opened books and half-read newspapers on every surface, a desk strewn with bills and the air heavy with tobacco smoke.

Today her father had an unlit cigar in his hand, not a brandy glass, and he was smiling. A good day, then. She released the breath she had not been aware she was holding, and moved forward to curtsy first to Papa and then, with a shy smile, to Richard. His own answering smile warmed her heart. His pleasure at her acceptance had never been in doubt.

"Well, Rosie, this is good news," Papa said. "You will not want to marry too quickly, not while you are still in black gloves, but Richard has said you may set whatever date you choose and he will not rush you."

"Mr Dalton is all consideration," Rosamund said.

"You have had two grievous losses this year," Richard said. "I should like to send the notice to the newspapers, but if you wish to delay the wedding until the spring, or even the summer—"

"How about February?" Rosamund said. "That will give me three months to get my wedding clothes, and I shall be quite out of black gloves by then."

"That would be delightful," he said, a hint of surprise in his tone.

But really, what need was there for delay? Now that the decision was made, it was as well to get the business over and done with as early as possible.

"Excellent, excellent. We must look out some of your mama's jewellery for you, eh? Rig you out properly, you know," her father said, in the vague way that she knew meant that his thoughts were drifting to more important matters. "Let us have some champagne to celebrate, hmm? Rosie, pull the bell, there's a good girl."

The younger sisters were called in to hear the good tidings, the champagne was sent for, several bottles of the best quality for the family, and a couple of bottles of an inferior type for the servants' hall, Richard was invited for dinner that evening and after a little perfunctory conversation, Papa chased them all out of his book room so that he could settle down for the rest of the afternoon with the champagne.

"You realise he will be drunk before the second course is on the table?" Rosamund said in an undertone to Richard as she accompanied him to the door.

"I am used to him," Richard whispered back. "Let him enjoy celebrating in his own way. Rosamund, Aunt Mary would love you to visit. Can you get the carriage tomorrow, or shall I send ours for you?"

She hesitated. It was on the tip of her tongue to protest that it was no distance to walk, but the first visit to the Park as its future mistress must, she supposed, be worthy of a celebratory carriage ride.

"It is Annabelle's day for the carriage tomorrow, but she is only going to the circulating library in Brinchester. She can drop me at the Park for a couple of hours, if that will not try Miss Dalton's hospitality too far. What time would suit best?"

"Any time after noon." He raised her hand to his lips, then smiled at her, still holding her hand. "I shall see you this evening, my dear. And... thank you."

She smiled and blushed and curtsied, all at the same time, then laughed at her own confusion. Within moments he was gone, and she was left to reflect upon her change in circumstance, and to wonder whether she was happy or not.

~~~~~

Rosamund had always liked Westerlea Park, but as she approached it for the first time as the betrothed of the heir, she saw it with new eyes. The imposing porticoed entrance, the warmth of the stone, the perfect symmetry — of all this she would be mistress, in time. The thought was pleasing. Her own home at Woodside was all irregular wings and inconvenient quirks, with narrow stairs and rooms just a little too small and ill-furnished for style, but Westerlea Park was exceedingly elegant.

Miss Dalton was waiting to greet her, rushing down the steps unheeding of the cold, damp November air, the ribbons of her cap flying, before the carriage had even stopped moving.

"Rosamund! How delightful this is!" Through the carriage window, she called out, "Good day to you, Annabelle. How are you today? And your father is well, I hope?"

Annabelle made all the right responses, and before long the carriage was bowling off down the drive and Rosamund was being led, arm in arm with Miss Dalton, up the steps to the house.

"We are so pleased, my dear, you cannot imagine," she said, patting Rosamund's arm. "It is just as we have always hoped."

Rosamund wondered about that, for Richard's hopes had certainly been otherwise for a while, but she said nothing, for Miss Dalton's sincerity was obvious.

"You must come and see Anthony first, you know, and I daresay a certain other person will be there too, in hopes of seeing you, but after that we may disappear to my boudoir and have a lovely chat together."

Like Papa, Lord Westerlea had a book room, but it was as unlike Papa's as it was possible to be. It boasted a high, painted ceiling, modern furniture of the lightest, most ethereal kind, and a small collection of modern paintings, which were not much to Rosamund's taste although they were admired by those with artistic sensibilities.

Lord Westerlea had never taken much notice of Rosamund in the past, beyond the usual intercourse of neighbours. Being a baron, he was far above them in rank and fortune, and he was very different in temperament also, a man who lived in the country but had no interest in country pursuits. He neither hunted nor fished nor shot. He employed an agent to deal with his tenants. He was an aesthete who dressed fashionably and rarely left his own house, and Rosamund was not entirely sure how he filled his days.

Miss Dalton was correct in assuming that Richard would be with his father, for there the two of them were, standing in front of the fire looking as smug as could be, as though there were some great accomplishment in marrying off the eldest son and eldest daughter of two adjoining estates. Since neither Richard nor Rosamund had ever been minded to trip through the glittering saloons of London in search of a marriage partner, their union was almost inevitable. The only wonder was that it had taken them so long.

"Rosamund, my dear girl!" Lord Westerlea said. "What wonderful news this is, to hear that you have finally taken pity on my lovelorn son."

Lovelorn — perhaps not that, but he seemed gratifyingly pleased, which was perhaps close enough.

"Lord Westerlea," she said curtsying demurely. Then another curtsy to her fiancé. "Mr Dalton."

"Miss Winterton," he said, his bow as formal as hers.

"Come, come, that will never do!" Miss Dalton cried. "Richard, at least take Rosamund's hand."

So he did, with a friendly smile and a kiss pressed into her gloved fingers.

"There, that is much better. I declare, I am so pleased for you both that I hardly know which day of the week it is. You two were always made for each other, and you will get along famously together."

That much, at least, she could agree with. Theirs may not be a love match, but they had so much in common they could not fail to get on well. She could imagine them in twenty or thirty years time, settled into their comfortable rural existence and with not the least ambition to move into the wider world.

"So they will, so they will," said the baron. "I wish you both every possible happiness. Rosamund, tell your father that I shall call on him very soon to discuss settlements."

It was half an hour or more before the effusions of delight had diminished sufficiently for Miss Dalton to steal Rosamund away to her boudoir. This room, in a quiet corner of an upper floor, overlooked the woods in one direction and the peacock lawn and lake in another. It was quite the most ravishing view, and Rosamund had already decided that it would be hers, one day. Perhaps not for a great many years, but she was patient. Unlike the rest of the house, elegantly ornamental and without a comfortable chair anywhere, this was a room designed for ease, with over-stuffed chairs, deep rugs, and family remembrances on every surface. Rosamund felt entirely at home seated in the bay window looking down to the lake and sipping very good tea from the finest bone china.

"Anthony has already sent the notice to the Gazette," Miss Dalton said. "It will be pleasant for our friends to have some news to talk about that is actually new. I am sure nothing else of note has happened since Mr Cromwell left the neighbourhood."

She left the remark hanging in the air, but Rosamund had never been coy, so she merely laughed. "There is no need to speak roundabout to me, Miss Dalton. He is gone, and, on the whole, I am glad of it."

"On the whole?" There was an anxious note to the words.

"Oh, indeed, for he was such a fine looking man, was he not?" she said, laughing. "And so well-dressed, a veritable tulip of the *ton,* and such an excellent dancer. It was always a delight to stand up with him. His attentions increased my consequence wonderfully, so I did not choose to discourage him. But my affections were never engaged." As if she could ever admire a man who clearly valued his valet and his tailor above any other mortal.

"Ah. We feared that you were nursing a broken heart, for although you have the most placid nature, Rosamund, and never show extreme emotions, that does not make you incapable of them."

"As to the general case, I cannot say," she said. "In this particular case, however, I have no very strong feelings for Mr Cromwell. I could never marry so vain a man, although he is so *very* handsome." She laughed but Miss Dalton did not smile.

"We in this house are partial, I am sure, and see no fault in Richard, but it cannot be denied that he did not show to advantage alongside Mr Cromwell."

She paused, perhaps waiting for some answering sign of partiality from Rosamund, too, but Rosamund was hard put to it to oblige her. What was there to say about Richard? He was neither handsome nor fashionable, he was not a man of deep thought or wit, nor was he romantic or poetic. He was a gentleman, and of good habits, and that was all she asked of him.

In the end, she said, "In appearance, perhaps, Richard was the inferior, but one does not marry a man for his well-formed chin, the cut of his coat, or his ability to execute the steps of the cotillion stylishly." Especially when such a man neglects to make the offer, she thought waspishly.

This seemed to satisfy Miss Dalton, for she went on, "I must confess, we were surprised to hear that Richard had raised the subject of marriage with you in such an informal manner. He has never been of an impulsive nature, and such a spontaneous address seems quite out of character. On previous occasions, he approached the matter with the seriousness that an offer of marriage warrants. He told us beforehand of his intentions, chose the moment with care, and dressed with unusual meticulousness. But this seems almost frivolous, to make the offer on an accidental meeting while out riding. Ah, I see your smile, Rosamund. Not as accidental as it seemed, then?"

She would have liked to prevaricate, but, no matter how pleased he might be at the outcome, Richard could not be unaware of how he had been manipulated, and might very well say so to his aunt.

"I shall have no secrets from you, Miss Dalton," Rosamund said. "There comes a time in every girl's career when she wearies of the constant search for a husband. Five years I have been out. Five years of waiting to be asked to dance, of waiting for gentlemen to call, of waiting for an offer to be made. I am tired of waiting, tired of sitting about hemming nightgowns and handkerchiefs, when I might have an establishment of my own. Once I had made up my mind to it, there seemed no point in delay. I knew, since it was a Tuesday, that Richard would be riding across Rivers Common, so I set my horse that way. And when the conversation turned in a suitable direction, I explained to him how wearisome the chase had become to me, and told him that I was minded to accept the very next offer I received."

As an explanation, it hid more than was revealed. She said nothing of how dreary her own home had become since Mama had died last winter, followed by the worse blow of her brother's loss in the summer. There was no mention of her father, and his retreat from the sorrows of life by drinking himself into a stupor every night. And she said nothing of her two suitors. She had always had suitors, but these two were especially noticeable.

For a whole winter they had vied for her attention at balls and parties. During the spring, when mourning kept her at home, they had visited her at Woodside. And when she emerged from seclusion in the summer, they had fought for the right to arrange gentle outings and card parties suitable for a young lady still in half-mourning. Mr Lancaster, as rich as a duke. Mr Cromwell, as beautiful as a Greek god. Mr Lancaster, bless him, had proposed twenty times at least, before his mother had recalled him to Bath, to Rosamund's relief. Mr Cromwell, however, had not spoken at all, had, in fact, left without a word to anyone. Not that she had had the least desire to marry such a dandy, but he was a man of some consequence and it peeved her to have failed.

But these two had brought her to the realisation that she was idling away her best years. It was time for her to set aside the trivialities of spinsterhood, and take serious thought to enter the state of matrimony. And as soon as this idea occurred to her, there was Richard in her mind's eye — a neighbour and childhood friend, a solidly worthy man, kind and considerate, who would, in time, be a baron. Not that she was hankering for a title, but it was certainly a benefit to the match. Richard was neither as rich as a duke, nor as beautiful as a Greek god, but he had offered for her twice already, and could easily be brought up to scratch. As indeed he had been. She was rather proud of her stratagem.

Miss Dalton chuckled in delight. "Oh, Rosamund, you clever girl! Naturally he was induced to propose on the spot."

"I did not expect so instant a response," Rosamund said modestly. "It seemed to me that his inclination towards me was all in the past. My only hope was that my words might induce him to consider the matter afresh, and that in time he might very generously renew his addresses."

"All in the past? My dear Rosamund, whatever could make you suppose such a thing? Why, Richard has never looked at another woman, I assure you. Well... not for many years, you know. *That* was mere foolishness. Calf love. He has long had his eye fixed on you."

Sipping her tea calmly, Rosamund made no comment. Richard's prior attachment was rarely spoken of within the family, for it was one of Miss Dalton's own friends who had inspired his devotion, although it was unrequited. Rosamund was pragmatic enough not to mind. Richard had never loved her, and, for her part, she felt no deep love for him either. They were well suited, however, both in temper and in habits, both preferring the quiet of the country to the cacophony of London, and the regularity of the seasons and their appropriate activities to the constant search for novelty amongst the fashionable. She would even go so far as to call him a friend. Yes, they would deal together well enough.

2: Holly Lodge

"Are you quite sure about this, dearest?" Annabelle said to her sister one day. They were arranging each other's hair before dinner, the first time the two had been alone together since Rosamund's announcement.

Rosamund threw her an amused glance. "Richard, you mean? I was never so sure of anything in my life. Are you going to look at me with teary eyes, like Fanny, and tell me how sad it is not to be in love with one's husband?"

Annabelle laughed. "Hardly that. You have never been of a romantic inclination, and you and Richard have known each other for ever. It is an excellent match — a neighbour, of good character, well-respected, and with a title eventually, although that would not weigh with you. You are well suited in both position and temperament. However, one does feel that, with your looks, you might do better than Richard Dalton. Hold still, dearest, this part is tricky."

For a moment there was silence as Annabelle contrived a complicated arrangement with a bandeau and some silk flowers.

"Richard is a very good sort of man," Annabelle went on, adjusting a ringlet, "worthy and dependable, but not terribly exciting. It would comfort me to know that you are not settling for second best. You are not yet an old maid."

"Certainly not!" Rosamund said indignantly. "I do not regard Richard as second best. He is very much my first choice."

"Yet you refused him twice."

"The first time I was only eighteen and having a wonderful time, and not in the least minded to settle into wifely responsibilities. And the second time—" Ah, now that was harder to explain. "It was a little over a year ago, and there was some talk of going to London, do you remember? And so I thought, and this is very shallow of me, I thought I might have my visit to London first, and marry Richard after. But then Mama died, and… and then… then Jeremy…"

The sisters lapsed into silence. Mama's death had been a blow, but the loss of their only surviving brother was a wound too raw to be brought into daylight.

"I did wonder," Annabelle said diffidently, "if perhaps you were falling into matrimony because of Papa."

The two exchanged glances in the mirror. Without a word, Rosamund rose and Annabelle took her place on the stool to be primped.

"This used to be such a happy house," Rosamund said quietly, brushing out Annabelle's braids. "Papa has taken it hard. It is not the drinking that bothers me, for he takes himself into his book room after dinner and we do not see the worst of it. But these overnight stays in Brinchester have become more frequent lately. What does he do there? Do you suppose there is…" She lowered her voice, although they were alone. "…a woman?"

"A gaming den, more likely," Annabelle said, with a disparaging sniff. "Havelock says that when a man sometimes returns happy and sometimes not, it is most likely the result of gambling."

"She should not say such things to you," Rosamund said sharply. "Nor should you listen to backstairs gossip. It is not our business what Papa does. Not every man can be a pattern card of moral rectitude."

"Very few of them are, from my observations," Annabelle said, with all the accumulated wisdom of her eighteen years. "Every man has some imperfection inside, like a worm in the apple, however unblemished the outward appearance may be."

"That is a very cynical view," Rosamund said, her hands stilling momentarily. "Most men are good-hearted, I am sure, and if they have been raised as gentlemen, then their flaws are bound to be very minor offences."

"Every man, high or low, is capable of the worst kind of depravity, if they have not great strength of character," Annabelle said in ominous tones. "Why, such a man might even slurp his tea! Think of that!"

And the sisters fell into peals of laughter, and all serious talk was at an end.

~~~~~

Rosamund found that her consequence was greatly increased by her betrothal. Dowagers who had taken little notice of her before now paid calls on her, and every starchy matron in the county wanted her presence at their dinner table. As a future baroness, she was someone to be taken notice of, it appeared. She rather enjoyed the attention.

Her life was busier, and visits between Woodside and the Park were more frequent, but otherwise her days went on much as before, with their rounds of calls made and calls returned, dinners given and attended, and hours spent plying her needle or practising the harp, just as always. And just as always, she was accompanied everywhere by at least one or two of her sisters.

Or almost everywhere. Only when she rode were they left behind, for Rosamund was the only one of the sisters who enjoyed the exercise. She rode everyday, whatever the weather, and hunted as often as possible, and nothing gave her greater pleasure than a day of hard riding over the fields and through the woods of Brinshire. For those few hours she was not Miss Winterton of Woodside, but just another rider who would follow wherever chance took her, and had no thought in her head but the next field or gate or ditch, and how best to get her horse and herself across. It was one of the many interests she shared with Richard, for he loved country pursuits just as she did. For those few hours she was free of the constraints of society, and free of the constant company of her sisters.

"It is very tiresome never having you to myself," Richard said to her one evening after dinner at Woodside. "You do not need to be chaperoned any more, Rosamund. You could spend five minutes alone with me without precipitating the end of times. Could we not sit in the morning room for a while?"

She smiled. "Whatever for? We may talk perfectly comfortably here, with a good fire blazing and plenty of light, and company about us if we run out of conversation ourselves."

He sighed. "You will ride tomorrow, I take it? The rain will not deter you?"

"It never has before. You will come round for me at eight, as usual?"

"Of course. Perhaps you might leave your groom behind, for once. You will be quite safe with me."

"Great heavens, Richard, ride out without my groom? Whatever will people say of me?" She laughed, but his face remained set and unsmiling, so she patted his hand gently. "When we are married, such liberties will be perfectly permissible," she said in what she hoped was a conciliatory tone.

"That day cannot come too soon," he said sullenly.

It was flattering to see him so eager, but she was not sure why he was so cross about it.

She began to get some inkling of his reasons when she was at the Park one day. She and Miss Dalton had been to Brinchester to see about wedding clothes, and Richard was on the step to greet the carriage as it arrived.

"Will you come in for a little while, Rosamund? For some tea, perhaps?"

"I am not sure... Papa will be expecting me. And Mrs Frith may call today."

"You can spare me half an hour, surely. I hardly ever see you these days."

"You came for dinner last night," Rosamund said, puzzled. "I shall be here for dinner tomorrow. Will you expire from disappointment if I do not drink tea with you in the meantime?"

"Half an hour, Rosamund."

There was a brusque tone to his voice that unsettled her a little, but she could not refuse him. And so she had had no choice but to go in, with all the bother of sending the horses round to the stables, only to be called out again in half an hour. And then he insisted that Rosamund divest herself of her pelisse and bonnet.

"You will not be comfortable otherwise," he said.

Then they sat, the three of them, Rosamund, Richard and Miss Dalton, making the most insipid conversation imaginable.

After a few minutes, Richard turned the conversation to the matter of the new carriage, already being built. "There are some samples of fabrics for the squabs about the place. Aunt Mary, would you mind fetching them for me? They will be in the drawing room... or perhaps the book room."

Miss Dalton looked uncertainly from one to the other. It was blatant, of course, for the house was full of servants perfectly capable of fetching whatever was required, but clearly Richard wanted to be alone with Rosamund.

"It is quite all right, Miss Dalton," Rosamund said. "We are betrothed, so there can be no impropriety in a few minutes alone."

With an anxious nod, she left, and Rosamund saw how she had been played from the smirk of satisfaction on Richard's face. He set down his tea cup, moved decisively to sit beside her on the sofa, and coiled one arm around her waist. Before Rosamund had time to make any protest, he had clamped his lips firmly on top of hers.

She had often wondered what it would feel like to be kissed. A few years ago, when she had been passing through the shrubbery near the kitchen door, she had observed the kitchen maid being thoroughly kissed by the footman, and they had both seemed to enjoy the business rather a lot. She had taken pains to pass through the shrubbery quite frequently after that, but had not seen them again, to her disappointment. The kitchen maid had left quite suddenly not long afterwards, and there had been no kissing to be seen anywhere after that.

It was not unpleasant, that was her first thought. Richard's lips were warm, and there was a masculine scent about him that she rather liked. He smelt of soap and horse, with a faint muskiness that was all his own. It was rather shocking to be embraced so unexpectedly, so *forcefully*, but his ardour was rather pleasing. She tried kissing him back, and he responded with even more force. When Miss Dalton returned and they jumped apart, Rosamund was left trembling and unsettled.

~~~~~

The wedding date was fixed, the wedding clothes and new carriage were in preparation, and the settlements were drawn up by the lawyers. Rosamund had no notion how much her dowry was to be, but Richard seemed rather pleased about it.

Her father, however, seemed less pleased. He was never happy when dealing with lawyers and bankers and others of that ilk, so the meetings for the settlements left him in high temper, his consumption of brandy alarmingly high. Even more worrying to his daughters, their mother's jewellery was nowhere to be found. Papa had searched the house from top to bottom, and had even ripped up floorboards and torn away wall panelling in Mama's room, but to no avail. Mama's family had been famous jewellers at one time, before they had given up the trade and become respectable, and she was rumoured to have brought a fortune in diamonds and emeralds and rubies to the marriage. Not that the sisters had ever seen any of it, apart from a necklace or two.

"And now it seems we never will," Lucy said mournfully.

Rosamund and Richard were to make their home in his family's dower house, known as Holly Lodge, which had stood empty and forlorn in the centre of Frickham village for some years. It had at one time been the lodge house for the Park, but when the new house had been built for the first Lord Westerlea, the present baron's father, a more grandiose entrance had been constructed outside the village, and the old entrance had been closed up, except for a small gate for the convenience of the servants.

Lord Westerlea had spared no expense in fitting up the house for his heir and his bride. Painters and carpenters were sent in first, and then a succession of carts arrived from

Brinchester bearing rugs and tables and beds and armoires and consoles and linens and silverware and china. Everything was new and expensive and fashionable. Rosamund had had very little to do with it, apart from an occasional trip to Brinchester to choose between one style or another. She soon learnt, however, that whenever she said, "This one is pretty," Lord Westerlea would say, "Do you think so? In my opinion, it is a little insipid. Now this, on the other hand..." So it was easiest simply to say, "What do you think, my lord?"

It was strange to her to find a man so interested in furnishings, but Lord Westerlea had very decided tastes, and she did not mind so very much what the house looked like so long as it was hers. She could always make changes later.

Six days before the wedding, she was at the Park making some last-minute arrangements with Miss Dalton. When it was time for her to leave, Richard said, "Shall I call for the carriage? Or perhaps you might like to walk, with my escort? It is such a fine day."

"That would be very pleasant. Thank you, Richard."

"If you do not dislike the idea, we might walk back through the village, and call in at Holly Lodge on our way. It will be our last chance to see it empty. We can have a quiet wander around by ourselves and look in all the rooms before the servants move in. Besides, our guests will start arriving tomorrow and we shall not have a moment to ourselves. You will enjoy that, Rosamund, and the extra distance is nothing at all. You will not be the least fatigued by it, I am sure."

Rosamund had spent long hours in the house already, and would no doubt be much occupied with showing visitors around it in the days to come, but she smiled and agreed to it. It was an excuse for more kisses, she supposed, and she could hardly object to such enthusiasm from her future husband. Her own enthusiasm was rather less than his, and she was beginning to rather dislike the way he seized every opportunity to get her on her own, and then pressed himself on her with some urgency.

They walked down from the Park together, skirting the lake and then through the old rose garden, rather desolate at this time of year. This small piece was all that remained from the old gardens that had surrounded the long-gone manor house. In four or five months the roses would be a blaze of colour, but just now winter still clung tenaciously to them, and it would take a perceptive eye to see the first shoots of spring emerging from the branches amidst the detritus of last year's glory.

"Shall you hunt tomorrow?" Richard asked. "You usually do, but perhaps you are too busy with wedding preparations just now?"

"I cannot imagine any aspect of the wedding that would keep me away from a hunt," she said, laughing. "Have no fear, I shall be there."

"Good, because it will be our last chance to escape before my step-mother and brother arrive."

"What is he like, your brother?" Rosamund asked.

"I have not seen him for years. He rarely comes here and I rarely go to London, but he was not promising, the last time I had occasion to meet him. I have no idea why he is coming at all."

"Why, he wants to see you marry, I daresay," Rosamund said. "It shows a very proper family feeling."

Richard gave a sound that was suspiciously like a snort of derision. "Not he! Who travels such a distance merely for a wedding? We were obliged to notify him and his mother of the event, of course, but no one suspected they would come. They are to stay for a month, too."

"If they have come all the way from London, they will hardly turn round and go straight back again," Rosamund said, amused, wondering why Richard was so put out. "I shall be very happy to make their acquaintance, for I do not suppose we shall ever go to London to visit them there."

"It is hard to think of a reason why anyone should, when one might live here in such pleasant country, and breathe good, clean air. The season does not appeal to me at all. So much expense, and all for show. We are better off here. Ah, I see the gardeners have been here, and tidied up a little."

They entered the grounds of the Holly Lodge through a small gate in the Park wall. Richard produced a key and unlocked the scullery door at the back of the house.

"No need to walk all the way round to the front, is there?" he said. "We do not want half the village knowing our business."

She thought it odd, but said nothing. Perhaps he was superstitious about entering together through the front door before they were married. She had known Richard all her life, but she never quite knew what he was thinking, and at such times he felt like a stranger to her.

They passed through the kitchen with its array of gleaming new pans, and along a passageway until they gained the hall.

"We can leave our coats here," Richard said blithely.

"Do you want us to freeze?" Rosamund said. "There are no fires lit."

He looked her up and down thoughtfully, then said, "Very well, leave your coat on if you wish, but at least take your bonnet off. And your gloves. I should like to hold your hand, my dear."

"Richard…"

"To please me," he said, with a grin, and running a finger down her cheek, bringing it to rest on her lips.

They walked slowly from room to room, sitting on the chairs, admiring vases and paintings and glass cabinets filled with china figurines, fingering the chess pieces already laid out on the board, although neither of them played. Richard's book room was already filled with books, and a pianoforte filled the designated music room. Rosamund wondered where she would be able to put her harp.

She was uneasy, although she could not say why. Richard was such a familiar face in her life, and had hardly changed over the years, but now there was a strange excitement in him. He insisted on trying every chair in the dining room, although they were all identical, and then he would look in every cupboard. She followed him in silence, waiting for the moment when he would lead her to a sofa for a kiss. But the moment never came.

Eventually they came back to the hall.

"Just the bedrooms to see," he said, grinning at her. "Shall we go up?"

"There is nothing of interest upstairs," she said. "One bedroom is much like another."

"I should like to see *your* bedroom," he said, with a meaningful look.

"Richard..."

"Such reluctance in a bride is unbecoming. Come, Rosamund." He took her hand firmly in his, and meekly she followed him up the stairs. He knew which room it was, for he took her straight there, ushered her inside and shut the door.

She walked across to the window, looking out over the little garden to the wall that marked the perimeter of Westerlea Park, and beyond it the ha-ha and lawns, although the house itself was out of sight. Every morning she would wake to this view, watching the changing seasons year after year. This was all her life held, now.

"Come here," he said softly.

She turned and looked at his excited face, his glittering eyes, and tried to reconcile this stranger with the restrained, gentlemanly figure she had known all her life. She made no move, and with a huff of impatience he crossed the room.

"Really, Rosamund! Why so coy all of a sudden, when you have been enticing me for weeks?"

And then the kisses came, more forceful than ever. Her lips were crushed, and his arms tightened painfully around her, squeezing her against his chest.

"Richard, I—" she said, as soon as he paused for breath.

"Hush," he said, pulling her away from the window and closing in for another kiss. "There is no need to wait, is there?" He began to back her towards the bed. "We are as good as married already."

She pushed against his chest. "Richard, no!"

His face was flushed, and there was an implacable look in his eye that frightened her. When he spoke, his voice was harsh.

"You have tormented me for too long, Rosamund. It is more than a man can bear. You are mine at last, and I will not be denied."

She closed her eyes and submitted to his will.

3: The Hunt

At least she did not have to go through the village. Richard walked her home on the path just inside the walls of the Park, silent but, when she dared to look at his face, glowing with exuitation. From there, they crossed the farm lane to the gates of Woodside. Here he bowed, kissed her hand and then, laughing, stroked her cheek.

"Dear Rosamund," he murmured. "Thank you for allowing me such pleasure."

Then he turned and walked away without a backward glance.

She hurried up the drive, then, not wanting to meet anyone, she ran round to the garden door and up the back stairs to her room. Flinging off her clothes, she scrambled into a nightgown, rang the bell and climbed into bed.

"You rang, miss?" Surprise in her tone.

"I am not well. Tell Mrs Thompson I shall not be down for dinner. I should like a tray here. Soup, and a jelly, perhaps."

"Very well, miss."

And then blessed silence.

Annabelle crept in once, left a cup of tea beside the bed, adjusted curtains and shutters, put more coals on the fire and then crept out again.

By the time her supper tray arrived, Rosamund had begun to feel that she was making too much of the incident. It had been unexpected, that was all, but it was no more than her marital obligation. If Richard had wanted to anticipate the wedding by a few days, there was no harm in that, was there? His eagerness was flattering. Perhaps she was mistaken in supposing him to be as coolly pragmatic about the marriage as she was herself. Had he been nurturing a secret passion for her all these years? He was a reserved and inarticulate man, so perhaps he had never been able to express his more tender feelings.

So she ate her supper, ordered a bath to be prepared for her and then returned to bed in a more composed frame of mind. She chided herself for her foolishness. It was not like her to be so missish! She would have to grow accustomed to these intimate encounters, and to seeing Richard in an entirely new light. He was no longer just a comfortable friend, he was soon to be her husband, and she must adjust her ideas of him accordingly.

Even so, when she woke the next morning, she was not quite easy with the prospect of joining him in the hunt. Would he look at her differently, with that oddly exultant expression? Would he be silent, as on the walk home? She could not bear his silence. How much easier it would be to meet him again first in the drawing room amidst a chatter of conversation, or even at church for the wedding, when any bashfulness on her part would be easily explained. For she would blush when she saw him again, she was quite certain.

With the decision to avoid the hunt made, she ordered breakfast in bed, and then settled down with a novel to while away the morning. Her peace was not to be undisturbed, however. One by one, her sisters peered round the door to enquire after her. It seemed pointless to lie in bed all day, for she was perfectly well, was she not? After another bath, she dressed carefully and made her way downstairs to join her sisters in the morning room.

Later, the Claremonts called, to enquire excitedly about the wedding preparations, and the Bowen brothers from High Frickham, former suitors of Rosamund's, bringing their young ladies for her inspection, which was rather sweet.

The callers had left and the dressing gong had already sounded when a horse was ridden rather fast up the drive, slithering to a halt in a shower of gravel.

"Groom!" the rider yelled. *"Groom!"*

Feet running on the gravel, then the sound of boots thundering up the steps and into the hall past Havelock. The sisters were half way up the stairs to dress for dinner, but they stopped, turned and stared at the newcomer. He was the eldest son of the Claremonts, their neighbours to the north, he was muddied to the eyebrows and was that blood on his coat? Had he come direct from the hunt? Rosamund was filled with a terrible dread.

"John? Whatever is the matter?" she said sharply, descending to meet him.

"Oh, Rosamund! I am so very sorry."

Somehow, even though she knew exactly what he was about to say, she was icily calm. "What has happened?"

"It is Richard — he was thrown at Whitebridge, that huge gate. The horse baulked, tossed him off and— I am so sorry!"

"Then... he is dead?" she whispered.

"I am so very sorry."

~~~~~

Rosamund hardly knew what she was doing. The circumstance was too dreadful even for tears. So close to being a wife and now... nothing.

While John Claremont went to the book room tell her father the news, her sisters led her, unresisting, into the morning room, where a fire still burned. Annabelle fetched brandy for her, Fanny, weeping, hugged her, Lucy held her hand, and Margaret sat at her feet in silent sympathy.

"Am I supposed to go into mourning?" Rosamund said. How strange that that should be the thought uppermost in her mind.

"Oh, how awkward," Annabelle said. "Another week and he would have been your husband, and a year would have been expected of you. But a betrothed... that is very awkward."

"There ought to be *some* observance," Lucy said.

"Miss Wilkes was so sad that she went into mourning for a year when her young man was killed in the Peninsula," Fanny said.

"Yes, but she was soundly ridiculed for it," Annabelle said. "Everyone agreed it was excessive. Miss Coates did not wear black at all, and was dancing again within a fortnight."

"There could not have been any great affection in the case," Fanny said sorrowfully. "Was there any censure?"

"No, for she had six younger sisters awaiting their turn," Annabelle said. "It was better for her to wed as soon as she could, the world understood that."

"The world is very cynical," Fanny said with a sigh.

"I must wear full black for a while, at least," Rosamund said, with sudden decision. "Until after the funeral, certainly. But then... I shall do whatever seems best to me at the time."

"It will depend on how desolate you feel," Fanny said.

Rosamund did not feel at all desolate. Sorry, of course, and not just for herself. She had lost the happy future she had envisaged with Richard, but perhaps in time there would be a happy future with another gentleman. But Lord Westerlea had lost his heir and Miss Dalton a beloved nephew. How distraught they must be! She would have to pay them a condolence visit in time, but she could hardly bear the thought of it. Their grief would be too painful to bear, and perhaps they would expect her to show the signs of grief, too, and she was not sure that she could. Her own sorrow was nothing to theirs. She could not be certain, for her emotions were churning so much she was dizzy, but she rather suspected that her overriding feeling was relief. And then she was ashamed of herself.

Her father sent for her, pacing back and forth in his book room. Surprisingly, there was an unlit cigar in his hand, rather than a brandy glass. He was in a good mood then?

"Well, this is a bad business, Rosie. I am glad to see you are not prostrate with grief. No woman looks well when her eyes are red with weeping. But you were always a sensible girl. You will have to be secluded for a while — a month or so should do it — but then you will have the summer, and you must look about you for someone else. You have had suitors enough, heaven knows. Look at this rug." He waved one hand towards it, and laughed. "Quite worn out by the feet of all the ardent young men wishing to pay their addresses to you." He chuckled. "Not everyone will be saddened by Richard's death."

"Papa!"

"Oh, I know. It is too soon to speak so. But you are one and twenty now, so—"

"Two and twenty, Papa."

"Is it so? Gracious, how the years fly by. Well, there you are, then. No time to be lost. Stay quietly at home for a few weeks, and then... back into the fray, eh? And you have all your wedding clothes already, so there need be no further expense."

"Lord Westerlea paid for a great many of them," Rosamund said.

"Doubtless he will forget about that, with so much else on his mind. No need to remind him, is there?" He chuckled. "Off you go, then. I daresay dinner has had to be put back, but tell Havelock not to delay too much. I am sharp set today. Close the door on your way out."

So she went, puzzled by his cheerfulness, but setting it down to some inscrutable male reason, to do with honour or money or business of some sort.

~~~~~

The ladies of the neighbourhood were too correct to visit the Park until the distress of the funeral had been overcome, but they could and did descend on Woodside to offer their condolences to Rosamund, and, she suspected, to observe how grief-stricken she appeared to be. She had no tears to display, but she hoped that her black gown and her pale composure would satisfy them.

"You are a sensible girl, Rosamund," Mrs Claremont said. "It reassures me to see you bearing up so bravely, in such trying circumstances. Not like Matilda Wilkes, the silly chit. To pretend to such grief, when she had only known the man for five weeks, and they were not even officially betrothed. Whereas you have known Richard Dalton for ever, so it would not be surprising if— But no matter. I am pleased to see you so calm. And perhaps the situation is not irretrievable."

"I do not understand you, madam," Rosamund said.

"No need to be missish," Mrs Claremont said, chuckling. "You must have noticed that Lord Westerlea has another son. And how convenient that the carriage is made, the settlements agreed, all the wedding clothes prepared." She smiled and patted Rosamund on the knee, whispering, "Do not worry, my dear, it is just my little joke. But you must agree, it would be the most convenient thing in the world, would it not? However, I will not tease you about it just now."

Rosamund was so astonished at this idea that she was rendered speechless. She soon found that Mrs Claremont was not the only one who saw the advantage in marrying Rosamund off to the younger son, now that the elder had inconsiderately died before the wedding. The others were more diplomatic, however. After expressing her condolences, Mrs Sheridan said, "We hear that Lady Westerlea and Mr Robin Dalton are visiting the Park just now. That must be a great comfort to Lord Westerlea and Miss Dalton, and how fortunate that they should be staying at such a time. Have you seen anything of them since their arrival?"

"No, nothing at all," Rosamund answered. "I have not seen either of them since they quit the county fifteen years ago."

Mrs Sheridan said, "Oh," in a tone of some disappointment.

"They arrived only on the day of Richard's death," Rosamund said, feeling some urge to explain. "Naturally they do not pay or receive calls yet."

"Not in the usual way, but you are an exception, surely? Still, I daresay once the funeral is over, you will meet them soon enough."

Rosamund shook her head. "I doubt it. Surely they will return to London at once?"

"Oh, no, they are to stay a whole month," Mrs Sheridan said triumphantly. "Mrs Carter had it from Mrs Smith, whose cook has a nephew who is a footman at the Park. Lady Westerlea has brought her own physician with her and has not yet recovered from the exertions of the journey, so it is quite certain not to be a short visit. You will meet them very soon, to be sure."

Rosamund was not so sure. Miss Dalton had written a tear-stained note to her expressing her sorrow that the happy day so long anticipated would not now take place, and Rosamund had replied in more restrained terms, and that surely would bring her association with Westerlea Park to an end. Although Lord Westerlea and Miss Dalton had always been most amiable, they had never distinguished her in any way until her betrothal to Richard. He alone had been her connection to the Park, and now that he was gone, she would not meet the Daltons except in the way of neighbours, with fifteen-minute morning calls, or at a dinner or card party now and again.

So she was astonished when, on the day before the funeral, Havelock informed her that Lord Westerlea and Miss Dalton were waiting to see her privately in the music room. The drawing room was rather crowded that day, for many friends and neighbours had called, but Havelock whispered discreetly in her ear and quietly she rose and followed the housekeeper out of the room.

The music room was not much used unless they were hosting an evening entertainment, but a fire had been hastily lit and the two stood huddled over the flames, Miss Dalton weeping softly, and Lord Westerlea grim-faced.

As soon as she entered, Miss Dalton fell on her, bursting into hysterical sobs. Rosamund embraced her gently, patting her shoulder.

"Oh, this is dreadful! Quite dreadful!" Miss Dalton said.

"Madam, pray let me send for some brandy," Rosamund said. "Or a glass of Madeira."

"No, no! I shall be better directly. Do not let me distract you from your talk with Anthony."

Rosamund turned and made her curtsy to Lord Westerlea.

"My dear Rosamund," he said, taking her hand as soon as she had risen. "How are you bearing up in these darkest of days?"

"My lord, it is I who should ask you that question. I cannot imagine how much you must be suffering."

"I do not understand it, Rosamund!" he burst out. "You knew Richard better than anyone. Was he not the most accomplished horseman? How could he fall so fatally? I cannot make sense of it."

"It was the Whitebridge gate, was it not? It is one of the most difficult hereabouts. The approach, the awkward lie of the land — it is very easy to get it wrong. Even an experienced rider may make a mistake now and then, and when one falls — there is always a risk. I would go so far as to say that the risk is part of the challenge of hunting. It adds to the enjoyment."

"But he was not *at* the gate! He was well short of it. No one saw what happened, for he was already on the ground when he was noticed, but he could not have been attempting the jump."

"My lord, a horse may startle at anything, and surprise even an expert rider."

"Then you do not see anything untoward about his death?"

She paused, considering. "Deaths on the hunting field are not uncommon, my lord," she said cautiously. "Why, only last year, Lord Wilman—"

"Lord Wilman was a fat fool who barely knew one end of a horse from the other, even when sober, which he seldom was. Richard knew what he was doing, but he was upset that day for some reason, or so I have been told. And you were not there. Had you quarrelled?"

Rosamund flushed. That was an uncomfortable question! But Miss Dalton placed a hand placatingly on her brother's arm. "It is not Rosamund's fault, Anthony. I expect she was unwell. Ladies do have days when they are not well."

He rubbed a hand across his brow, and she saw the strain on his face. Poor man! He had lost his eldest son and heir, so naturally he was devastated. He hardly knew what he was saying.

"I beg your pardon, Rosamund. Of course I did not mean to imply—" He waved a hand vaguely towards some chairs. "Will you sit? For I have a matter I would discuss with you."

She sat, perched awkwardly on the edge of a chair, wondering what on earth Lord Westerlea could possibly wish to discuss with her.

"Rosamund," he said, and for the first time she saw nervousness beneath the suave exterior. Lord Westerlea nervous? What could it possibly mean? "My dear girl, you must be aware of how... how *delighted* we were when you betrothed yourself to Richard. Nothing could have been better calculated to please us. A neighbouring family, and we know you so well. You are not some silly chit of a girl without a thought in her head. As I said to Richard, if I had sketched out my ideal woman for him to marry, do you see, you would have fitted the image to perfection. Who could be better suited to be mistress of Westerlea Park?"

"My lord, I thank you for the compliment, but—"

"Hear me out, pray. But now fate has intervened. Your marriage to Richard is not to be. But—" He stopped and again ran a hand across his brow. He looked at her, took a breath, then slowly exhaled. Then, as if deciding to tackle the most challenging jump straight away, he rushed on, "Rosamund, I have another son. No, please, let me have my say. He is to stay with us for a month, for my wife cannot contemplate the return journey to London sooner, and therefore there is time for you to get to know him. It may be, do you see, that you would find him to be just such another as would make you an admirable husband."

"My lord—"

"I know, I know. Every feeling revolts against the idea of contemplating matrimony again so soon. But there need be no rush, not the least hurry in the world. You have this month to get to know each other, and who knows what might develop? And everything is already arranged for the marriage in such a satisfactory way. It would be such a shame to waste all our efforts, do you not agree? Will you at least meet him and see if anything takes? To please me? For I should so like you to be part of the family."

She could hardly refuse, although it was the last thing she wanted. "I will meet Mr Dalton, my lord."

"Excellent, excellent! You will find him to be the best of fellows. I shall send the carriage for you on Thursday at noon. Come, Mary. Let us leave Rosamund in peace now. Pray give my regards to your father."

So saying, they swept out, Miss Dalton still sniffing into her handkerchief, leaving Rosamund to contemplate the extraordinary proposal in bemusement.

4: The Library

Robin Dalton stared out of the window at the relentless rain. Such dreary weather, but all of a piece with his mood. It was bad enough to be dragged to this God-forsaken piece of England for a wedding, but to find himself attending his brother's funeral instead was too dispiriting for words. And now he found himself elevated to the position of heir and all the comfort of his life was over. He could no longer spend his days pleasantly in London, unnoticed and unregarded, but would be expected to learn about tenant farmers and cottage roofs and the management of cattle and other such horrors. All while wading ankle deep in mud, no doubt. He shuddered.

And now he was to have his brother's wife foisted on him, some rustic little country mouse, no doubt. Not actually his brother's wife, unfortunately. If only Richard had survived just a few days more! Then he would have been married, this Miss Winterton would be his widow and the church would frown on any question of marriage between her and Robin, and he would be safe.

Still, it was only for a month. His father had already agreed that he might return to London to fulfil his obligations during the season. He would meet this girl, to please his father, but there would be no marriage, on that he was determined. He had not yet met the lady who met all his requirements for a wife.

"Of what are you thinking, Robin dear?" His mother's voice was languid, as always. She never exerted herself, her tone such as to imply that even the effort of speech was almost beyond her. She never travelled without her personal physician, and yet her condition never improved.

"Of rain and mud and cows and peasant hovels," he said.

"Ah, yes. It would be insupportable to have to live here, where civilisation is but a distant memory."

"There is a circulating library in Brinchester, I believe," he said, crossing the room to the chaise longue where she reclined and sitting on a footstool beside her. "And assembly rooms, with a public ball once a month."

"Goodness, how thrilling," she said. "The natives must be quite exhausted with such dissipation."

He laughed. "Are you sure you wish to stay the full month, Mother dear? If we leave on Monday next, we could be home a week from today without pushing ourselves, and think how comfortable that would be."

"If your father were a more reasonable man, perhaps that would be possible, but it will take me at least the month to convince him to increase my allowance. He will refuse and refuse and refuse, seeing the end of our visit approaching, then I shall threaten to stay another month and he will agree to anything to be rid of me. We planned this very carefully, Robin dear."

"We did not plan for the wedding to turn into a funeral. To bury the man on the very day he was to have been married seems in poor taste to me, but there we are. Sensibilities are coarsened the further one gets from London."

"Very true. And you will have to be pleasant to this local girl — what is her name?"

"Winterton."

"Ah yes. I remember the Wintertons. From Woodside. An ugly little house. I will say this for your father, he has excellent taste. This house is quite elegant, and one would not be ashamed to entertain any of one's friends here."

"No, indeed. Father's taste is impeccable, a fact of which I was unaware."

"You were but seven when we left here," his mother said. "He has made great improvements since then, and added extensively to his collections. Perhaps that is why he is so penny-pinching these days."

A gentle scratching on the door announced one of the footmen. "Beg pardon, sir, but his lordship requests your presence in the library."

"Ah. My penance for the day. I shall see you later, Mother dear, after your rest." He bent to kiss his mother's powdered cheek and then followed the footman downstairs.

The library was one of the most imposing rooms at Westerlea Park, but since neither of its residents read a great deal, it was seldom used. Lord Westerlea had his book room and Miss Dalton her boudoir, and for entertaining, the saloon, drawing room and dining room served the purpose well enough. Had Lord Westerlea or his sister ever wished to hold a ball or musical soirée, there was a music room with several instruments and a gallery which made a tolerable ballroom. The library, with its high, decorated ceiling and double layer of bookcases generally sat empty and forlorn.

Now a good fire burned in the vast hearth, with Lord Westerlea warming his elegantly attired behind in front of it.

"Ah, Robin, my boy! Come in, come in. The carriage has gone out to fetch Rosamund, so she will be here in a few minutes. You will be kind to her? She has received a dreadful blow, and I daresay she does not know where to turn for comfort. I have sown the seeds of the idea, do you see, but the rest is up to you. You will give careful thought to the idea, my boy?"

"Of course, sir."

"She is a lovely girl, quite lovely."

"So you said, sir. I am all eagerness to meet such a beauty," he added politely.

"And a sensible girl. Nothing coy or frivolous about her. She understands the benefits of the alliance, you may be sure, and your manners, your appearance are such as must please any young lady, I am persuaded."

Robin bowed. "You flatter me, sir."

"Well, well. We shall see. All I ask is that you get to know her, and— Ah, I hear the carriage now. Wait here and I shall bring her to you."

He hurried out of the room. Robin strolled along the lower bookcases. One end of the room was filled with the dilapidated volumes brought from the old manor house. He had no interest in those. A couple of bookcases held new books, all pristine, sent by the box from London, he supposed. He selected one, cut the pages and settled down in a wing chair near the fire to read.

After a few minutes, the door opened. He carefully marked his place, set down his book and rose to his feet.

"Ah, Robin, my boy, there you are! Well, well. Here is Miss Winterton to meet you. Rosamund, my dear, may I present to you my younger— my son, Robin."

She was every bit as beautiful as his father had described. That was a surprise, although given his father's aesthetic sensibilities, perhaps it should not have been. He had supposed it to be mere hyperbole, a charitable depiction of a prettyish bucolic female. Instead he saw a very good-looking woman, almost as tall as he was, with a fine figure and regular features. Her skin was smooth and alabaster-white, her dark hair curled becomingly around her face, and her eyes — were they green? He rather thought they were. The pelisse and gown were plain, but with more stylish clothes she could certainly turn heads in London.

She curtsied demurely. "How do you do, Mr Dalton."

"It is a pleasure to make your acquaintance, Miss Winterton. My father has told me a great deal of you, and I can see that his description of your perfections was not exaggerated."

She bowed in acknowledgement of the compliment, but there was no hint of a blush or a consciousness. "Lord Westerlea has been less forthcoming to me, for he has told me nothing at all of you, Mr Dalton. Your perfections remain to be discovered."

That was a sharper response than he might have anticipated. Was she saying that his appearance was not perfect? That if he had perfections, they would need to be teased out? However he examined her words, he could not make them into a compliment.

But his father noticed nothing, and laughed merrily. "Well, well. I shall leave you two to get acquainted for half an hour or so. I will tell Barnaby to send in some tea."

When he had gone, Miss Winterton said, "He looks a little better today. I am glad he has you and Lady Westerlea here to raise his spirits, for I fear Miss Dalton's grief makes her poor company."

Robin said quietly, "I do not imagine any company can raise his spirits in such circumstances, do you? A man who loses his son must be distraught, with no comfort to be found anywhere. What more natural than to retreat from society?"

Her chin lifted at this mild reproof. "It is necessary to make the effort, however. Wallowing in grief is unwholesome. There is always comfort to be gained from the sympathetic presence of family or close friends, and if even that fails, there is the comfort of God."

Ah, yes, the unshakable faith of the country dweller. There was no harvest too poor, no season too wet or cold or hot or dry but one must give thanks to God for it. The peasant might be starving and yet would still walk to church twice on Sundays to thank God for his patch of foul mud and the crumbs on his table. There was no point talking theology to such simpletons, especially one who expressed her views so forcefully. It was time to get to the point.

"Miss Winterton, you are aware of my father's hopes for us, I understand?" She hesitated, then nodded. "You must be as uncomfortable as I with this plan. For myself, I have no intention of marrying for some years yet, and you must also have your own wishes on the subject, in which I play no part. I am sure you would prefer a husband from amongst your own kind, here in Brinshire. Yet one would not wish to disoblige a grieving father at such a time. These half hours when we are thrown together need not be onerous. There is no need for us to exchange any conversation. I have already selected a book to read. May I suggest that you do the same? Then we may sit quietly and not trouble each other."

"As you wish," she said coolly. Was he unduly sensitive or was there a hint of rebuke in her tone? Perhaps she was just naturally cold.

"The older books are over there, and the more recent works are in these cabinets here." He stood politely waiting while she looked about her.

"May I read the newspaper?"

"Of course," he said. "Do you not have any at home?"

"No. Papa does not hold with them," she said, her lips twitching into a half-smile. "There is nothing in them but war and battle and death and flood and pestilence, he says. He prefers novels, especially ones which end happily."

"Then pray, choose a newspaper and take your fill of battle and pestilence, Miss Winterton."

She sat, and then he was able to take up his volume again.

For some time he read, absorbed in his book.

The door opening startled them both. She gave a little gasp of surprise, and he lost his place in the book. She was restful company, there was no doubt about that, for his reading had not been disturbed in the slightest by her presence.

They both jumped up.

"Well, well," his father said, rubbing his hands together. "How are we getting along, now?"

"Perfectly well," he answered.

"We have not exchanged a single word of discord," she said blandly. Robin shot her a suspicious glance, but his father smiled and nodded.

"Excellent. And you will come for dinner tonight, Rosamund?"

She looked startled, throwing Robin a thoughtful glance, before she said, "Thank you, my lord, but my father will be expecting me home this evening."

"Hmm. Tomorrow then. I shall send the carriage for you at six. Robin, did you mention Richard's will to Rosamund at all?"

"The subject did not arise, sir."

"Well, well, I daresay you had better things to talk about. Rosamund, Richard had made a new will in anticipation of..." He paused, took a deep breath, then ploughed on, "That had to be set aside, of course, so the old will applied, but there was one bequest in the new will..." Again, emotion overcame him momentarily. "His horses," he rushed on. "He desired you to have his horses, and I should like to honour his wishes."

"Oh... but his hunters are very valuable, my lord. Do you not—?"

"No, no. I shall send them round to you this afternoon, and the groom. You must have them, my dear. I cannot bear to think of them in the stables... a constant reminder, do you see?"

"I shall be very happy to have them. You are very kind, my lord. Thank you." She dipped a curtsy, and Robin had to admire the precision of it, neither too deferential nor too familiar. Again, he was conscious of a desire to see her fashionably dressed and parade her through the ballrooms of London. Would she dance well? Her movements were graceful, so he rather thought she would display to advantage in the dance.

His father nodded approvingly. "Good, good. And you will come again to spend time with Robin? At noon tomorrow?"

A hesitation, and for the first time, her composure slipped. Then she mastered herself and said calmly, "Of course, my lord. I shall look forward to it."

"Excellent. The carriage is at the door, Rosamund. Give my regards to your father. Barnaby will show you out."

She disappeared after the housekeeper, and the door clicked shut again.

"Well? What do you think? Is she not a peach?"

"She is an attractive woman," Robin said.

"Attractive? Is that all you can say about her? You will not find many better looking even in London, I wager. And a sensible girl, no foolishness about her. She has been running her father's house for a year, since her mother died. A good manager, do you see? You could not do better, Robin."

"She is quite a paragon," he said dryly.

"Indeed she is, and not a hint of gossip about her. A good, virtuous girl."

"A state not likely to continue long if you allow her to be alone with me and quite unchaperoned," Robin said in some amusement.

"Well, well, but she is quite safe with you, my boy."

"Of course she is, but that is hardly the point."

"You have been too long in town, my boy. Around here, Rosamund is known and valued for her good qualities, and she does not lose her reputation by spending half an hour alone with a man she has known since childhood."

He did not press the point, but he wondered how virtuous a woman could be who made no protest about such seclusion. Country manners left much to be desired.

"She is possessed of one other great virtue which, perhaps, I should have mentioned earlier," his father said smugly.

"Indeed?" Robin said politely.

"A dowry of twenty thousand pounds."

"Twenty thousand! Good God! There are not many duke's daughters can boast so much. Winterton is not a nabob, is he? Or a cit?"

Lord Westerlea chuckled. "Not the least whiff of trade about *him*, my boy. The Wintertons have been gentry for generations. To be honest, I would not have supposed him to be worth so much, for he does not exactly splash the readies about, but I daresay it came from his wife. Her father was in the jewellery trade before he bought his estate, and she had some exquisite pieces tucked away, so it was said. Years ago, when the children were small, he promised me such a sum if I married Richard to Rosamund, and when the time came, he made good on his word. So you can see why it would be a desirable match for you, my boy. Richard was very pleased about it, I can tell you, for you need not imagine he was in love with the girl, or any such romantic nonsense."

"I should not have thought it would weigh with *you*, Father. You are not exactly in the basket."

"Not exactly, no, but this place is expensive to run, and then there is your mother. It is a consideration. It would give you a good independence, my boy."

"Yes, indeed. Although... one does not marry solely for money. There must be a compatibility, too."

"Of course, of course. No one will force you into it. But if you should discover a liking for the girl...? Do you see?"

Robin did see. Twenty thousand pounds, and a face and form that would attract attention even in London... If only she were not such a cold, reserved creature, with those country manners. But his destiny lay elsewhere, he was sure of that, and especially now. He would be a baron one day, so surely he could look a little higher for a wife than Miss Winterton of Woodside.

~~~~~

"Well? What is he like?"

Four pairs of eyes gazed eagerly at Rosamund. What to say about Mr Robin Dalton?

"He is... very handsome." She could concede that much.

"Ooooh!" her sisters said in unison.

"More detail!" Lucy cried. "Is he short or tall? Dark or fair? Is he shy or forward?"

"He is of average height, I should say. Quite slim. His hair is fair. He is well-mannered, neither shy nor forward. And he dresses..."

"Yes?" they said.

"...like a coxcomb." She giggled. "You would have laughed if you could have seen him! His coat is tight-fitting everywhere, his shirt points are so high that his face is like *this*..." She tilted her face so that it pointed towards the ceiling. "...and as for his neckcloth! I never saw such a complicated arrangement."

"Was he as grand as Mr Cromwell?" Annabelle said. "He was always dressed very fine."

"Mr Dalton would cast Mr Cromwell quite in the shade, as far as finery is concerned," Rosamund said decisively.

"So you will not marry him," Fanny said sadly.

"Certainly not!" Rosamund said. "He is exactly the sort of man that I cannot like. His manners are formal and without warmth, and I cannot approve a man who clearly devotes so much time and effort to his appearance. It is a kind of vanity that I despise. One must take care with one's appearance, naturally, but there is a disagreeable conceit in any man who spends so much time before his own looking glass. No, I cannot like him, and I have not the least intention of marrying him, you may be sure of that."

Fanny sighed in disappointment.

"Besides," Rosamund said, "he was disparaging about the people of Brinshire. *'Your own kind,'* he said, as if we are a different species here, and he is too grand to mingle with the lower forms of life. Such disdain is offensive, and I cannot like him on that account alone. Such insufferable self-importance! No, I may safely promise you never to marry such a man."

5: A Proposal

"Is she quite dreadful?" Robin's mother said, when he visited her sitting room that afternoon.

"Not at all dreadful," Robin said. "If I could have the dressing of her, perhaps with the aid of your Madame Aubert, she would pass muster anywhere. Assuming she can dance, of course."

"Robin dear?" she said quizzically. "You are not developing a *tendre* for the chit?"

He laughed. "Certainly not. However, I could easily develop a *tendre* for her twenty thousand pounds."

His mother sat bolt upright. *"Twenty thousand?"*

"That drew my attention also. A tidy sum, is it not? I could almost tolerate her country manners for such a prize."

"But you would not have to," she said gleefully. "You could leave her here with her bucolic friends while you go on as before in London. Nothing could be more perfect. I must meet this Miss Winterton for myself."

"She is to come to dinner tomorrow night."

"Excellent. Robin, you must consider this carefully, for such opportunities are rare indeed. Twenty thousand pounds would set you up very comfortably, very comfortably indeed, and with your attractions you could secure her easily."

"I am not so sure about that. She is very cool towards me, and besides, she has just lost the man she was to wed. One must suppose her to have held Richard in affection. I do not imagine she is minded to marry at this present any more than I am."

"Still, you must make a push for her. Promise me you will try."

"I promise you I will consider the matter very carefully," he said, and with that she had to be satisfied.

Now that Robin was watching Miss Winterton with greater interest, he found much to admire in her, even beyond her twenty thousand pounds. Her gowns might not be the height of fashion, but in her mourning attire she looked perfectly the part for her place in society — restrained, demure and tasteful. At dinner, he discovered that she ate anything offered to her, could converse easily on any subject and was appropriately deferential towards her betters without servility. It was rather pleasing. Her mind was not well-developed but she was aware of her deficiency and readily deferred to his opinion on subjects where she was ill-informed. She showed great interest in his life in London, which he thought was not feigned, and he found himself talking to her quite freely.

She had a sharp tongue at times, though. When he had uttered some praise of the pork, she had said, "Our pigs grow well here. We have so much mud in the country, you see." And once, when he had described a leader of fashion in glowing terms, she had murmured, "How fascinating. Here in Brinshire, amongst my own kind, I have seen no such paragon."

Such wit showed a quickness of mind that he had not suspected in her. He was amused rather than offended, although it confirmed his view that she was not attempting to ensnare him, and was uninterested in matrimony. As was he, naturally, although the sum of twenty thousand pounds had begun to prey on his mind rather. What an inducement! He would have an income of his own, and no longer be dependent on his father for an allowance. His expenses would not be very much the greater by marriage, for she could live at Westerlea Park at his father's expense, and he would continue to live under his mother's roof. What could be more agreeable to all concerned? And so he began to see Miss Winterton in a different light.

~~~~~

The Woodside stables were become rather crowded, and the old pair of carriage horses, only used nowadays to pull the barouche in the summer, had been moved out to the hay store until some better arrangement could be contrived. Five hunters and three hacks had arrived for Rosamund, and Richard's groom, grey-faced with grief, to tend them.

"Well, Jed, you need not worry for your place," Rosamund said to him. "Papa has said you may stay with us for as long as you like."

"Will you sell 'em, miss?" he said anxiously.

"Not immediately." His face relaxed. "Blueberry Boy is coming to the end of his hunting career, and my own Larchpole is not far behind, so we may reduce the numbers by degrees, but there will be plenty of work for you for a while yet."

"It's not that, miss," he said. "I could get work no trouble. But Mr Richard loved those 'orses and I'd 'ate to see 'em split up and sold away from 'ere."

"Even Heracles?"

"It weren't 'is fault Mr Richard broke 'is neck," Jed said stoutly.

There was no answer to that. "Why did his lordship send all the saddles?" she asked.

"Jus' wanted rid of 'em, I guess," Jed said.

"I have no use for them. The other tackle, possibly, but— oh, this rein is broken."

"Aye. That was what was on 'eracles that day," Jed said. He scuffed his feet, and added, "I s'pose Mr Richard must 'ave broke it when 'e fell."

"That must be it," she said, but she looked at the cleanly snapped leather and wondered at it. It did not look like any accidental breakage such as she had seen before. "It could not be anything else, could it?"

"Course not, miss," Jed said at once, not quite looking her in the eye. "I'll get rid of it, shall I? It's no use now, is it?"

"That would be a waste of good leather," she said.

Jed nodded, and returned to his duties, and Rosamund was left standing in the stable yard, the broken rein in her hand. A dreadful thought had entered her mind, and once it was there it could not be banished. She could see that Jed had the same suspicion, but it was almost too terrible to contemplate. Was it possible that the rein had been deliberately cut through? And if so, by whom? Surely no one could have wished Richard any harm?

Only one person stood to benefit from his death, and that was Mr Robin Dalton, who was now heir to the barony and the wealth of his father's estate. Robin Dalton, who had never entered the county for close to twenty years, but had suddenly taken it into his head to visit now, just when his elder brother was about to marry. It was too coincidental for words.

With a wave of relief, she remembered that Mr Dalton had not even reached Westerlea Park until after the event. Richard had been already out with the hunt when Robin had arrived. It was all right, there was no question of murder, it was impossible. Her overwrought mind was putting foolish ideas into her head, and she determined not to mention such suspicions to anyone. She was not quite comfortable throwing the broken rein away or leaving it in the stables to excite speculation in others, so she hid it away in her stocking drawer.

Rosamund counted the days until Lady Dalton and her son would take themselves back to London and she would be plagued no more by their presence. Every two or three days, Lord Westerlea came up with some excuse to get her to the Park — to take tea with Miss Dalton, to join them for dinner, to admire a new painting, or simply to be shut away in the library with Mr Dalton for half an hour. She could not object, for her cooperation pleased his lordship, and Mr Dalton was not arduous company. When they were obliged to talk, he was an entertaining conversationalist and when they were not, he was peaceably silent, allowing her to read whatever she liked.

She enjoyed the dinners best, although with only six around the table, they were pleasant rather than lively. Lord Westerlea and Miss Dalton were amiable hosts, and Mr Robin Dalton had considerable powers of conversation. Lady Westerlea was a fashionably languid woman, who treated Rosamund with amused disdain. Miss Finch was a friend of Miss Dalton's, one of a succession of friends who bore her company for a week or two at a time. She was an angular woman dressed in black, who made Rosamund think of a spider. Mr Hathaway was Lady Westerlea's personal physician. His role seemed to be to sit beside his mistress and fuss over every bite of food she ate or did not eat, as he determined whether each dish might be beneficial or detrimental to her health. Yet despite all his efforts, it seemed to Rosamund as if she ate and drank precisely what she pleased.

When the ladies withdrew, Lady Westerlea reclined on a sofa and half-dozed until the gentlemen came through, while Miss Finch worked determinedly on her tatting. Miss Dalton was inclined to reminisce at length over Richard, recalling incidents from his childhood and youth that she could not possibly have remembered, since she had not moved to Westerlea Park until after Lady Westerlea had left and

Richard was quite well-grown. After the second evening of such dispiriting talk, Rosamund asked if she might play the pianoforte. It was not her favourite instrument, but anything was better than Miss Dalton's sugary remembrances.

When Mr Dalton joined the ladies, he came at once to the instrument. "A little music — how delightful! You play well, Miss Winterton."

"I thank you for the compliment, sir, but I fear you are a wicked flatterer. I am perfectly aware, for you have told me so yourself, that you have listened to some of the best performers in the land, those worthy to play even before members of His Majesty's own family. I may manage to strike the keys in more or less the proper order, but I do not pretend to reach any level of proficiency above the tolerably competent."

He laughed, and raised his hands in surrender to acknowledge the hit. She was struck by how handsome he was when he set aside the cold society carapace and allowed himself to display the man inside.

"I was taught never to quarrel with a lady, but in this case I must make an exception. Tolerably competent, indeed! I cannot allow it to be so. Your fingers may not fly over the keys quite as fast as with some performers I have seen, but the pleasure to the listener is every bit as great, I assure you, and that is no flattery at all. May I fetch you some more pieces from the music room? There is not much to choose from here."

"Thank you, but I believe your father wishes to play cards, and I should not like to disturb the play."

"Another time, I hope," he said, with a small bow.

She could not be displeased with such manners. It was all flummery, of course, but he displayed such an air of sincerity as almost to convince her that he was beginning to like her. As for him, she still despised the dandy in him, but he had a fine mind, was well-educated and showed a great deal of proper feeling. He was arrogant, naturally, but as the son of a baron, and one who moved in the upper echelons of society, that was only to be expected.

About three weeks after Richard's death, Rosamund was shown into the library for one of her regular half hours with Mr Dalton. She had grown accustomed to these visits, and had even begun to enjoy them rather. He often marked pieces in the newspaper that might interest her, and sometimes he would explain the background to them, so that she felt informed and could understand the nuances of the speech in Parliament or whatever it happened to be. But today when she arrived, he was not sitting reading in his chair as usual. Instead, he stood with his back to the fire, his face serious.

As soon as the housekeeper had withdrawn, he said, "Miss Winterton, would you be so good as to favour me with your attention for a few minutes? I have a matter of import to discuss with you."

Her heart sank, but he ushered her to a chair and began his speech.

"Miss Winterton, you may remember the occasion when we first met. My father introduced us in the hope that we would get along well enough to contemplate the possibility of resuming the alliance between our two families. I told you at the time that I had no thought of marriage for some years yet. I am, after all, only four and twenty."

She nodded, unwilling to interrupt him in mid-flow, but wishing with all her heart that she could prevent him from saying the words she now feared she was to hear. He was not in love with her, that much she knew. Enough men had looked at her with adoration in their eyes for her to recognise the signs, and in Mr Dalton she saw none of them. Nor was there the comfort of familiarity that she had enjoyed with Richard. Mr Dalton was a man she could respect for his good qualities, but he was too much the captive of society's judgement for her to like him. His clothes, his manners, his flattery were well-suited to London, his proper milieu, but she thought them foolish. She could never marry such a man, and she had thought herself the last person to attract his notice. What could possibly have changed his mind?

But she must let him have his say without interruption.

"Now that I have come to know you better," he went on, pacing about the room as he got into the spirit of his declaration, "I see that my father was quite right in his assessment of you. Your great beauty I could see at once, but your gentle nature, your good sense and your ease in society I very soon discovered. And beyond all these…"

She let his words roll over her head. It was all flummery, and he was so practised at it. But then came the point at which he should have enumerated the advantages of the match — the adjoining estates, the long-standing friendship between their two families, the elevation in rank which he could offer, his position in society and so on and so forth, before asking outright for her hand. But he did not.

Instead, he smiled and said gently, "In all this, I concur with my father's view of the matter. But as to marriage, my opinion is not yet settled. My father is a romantic. He sees that we readily converse when seated together at dinner, or when playing whist. He sees that I admire your beauty and respect your gentle nature, as any man must. He leaps from there to the idea of matrimony, and takes it as quite a settled thing. But I cannot be so confident of our compatibility. Even with such a short acquaintance, it is my fear that your amiable nature conceals such fundamental differences between us as would make such a course imprudent, that we are, perhaps, too unlike ever to be happy together. What is your opinion, Miss Winterton? Do you think that, in time, we might reach an accommodation sufficient to allow us risk a match between us, or should such an idea be given up at once?"

It was not quite the question she had expected, and in fact it was not a question at all. He wished only for her to agree with his opinion. Fortunately, his views exactly coincided with her own. "Mr Dalton, I am flattered by your good opinion of me, which I cannot feel I deserve. However, it seems to me that you are correct in supposing that we are too different ever to be well-suited. You move in such elevated society where I could never be comfortable, and our natures are so dissimilar that I am persuaded that you could never make me happy, sir, nor I you."

"I suspected you would say as much," he said, composedly. "I feared it might be so. It would delight me to respect my father's wishes in the matter, but such a course is not to be thought of, so let me tease you no more on the subject. I wonder if you have thought any more about the

Prime Minister's proposals that we discussed the other day? There is one interesting aspect that might not have occurred to you…"

Bemused, she listened to his calm words, and it was almost as though the conversation had never happened.

~~~~~

"So she would not have you?" Lady Westerlea reclined on a chaise longue in her sitting room, while Thomas Hathaway, her physician, massaged her feet to increase the warmth in them.

"No, Mother dear. She thinks me a fribble, I make no doubt, and despises me with every ounce of her country-bred heart."

"A fribble? And you a veritable pink of the *ton!*"

"One does one's best," Robin said modestly.

"Well, it matters not. Now you have done your disagreeable duty by the chit and obliged Anthony, and he will have no option but to increase my allowance. It was very bad of him to make the one contingent on the other."

"One cannot blame him for trying, and twenty thousand pounds would have relieved him of the necessity to do anything at all for you. It would have been a tidy increase in our income. However, it is a great relief that she was so decisive, and the business was not at all disagreeable, Mother dear. There is something to be said for forthright country manners after all, for she gave me no bird-witted foolishness."

A relief in some ways, but also somewhat chastening that she was not even slightly tempted. There was not a second's hesitation before she agreed wholeheartedly that they were not suited.

"She is a fool to turn you down," his mother said tartly. "She will not get a better offer."

"With her dowry she will not be short of offers," he said.

He decided not to mention that he had not, in fact, offered for her, but merely sought her opinion as to whether he should. He thought it rather a clever proceeding, for it satisfied his father's insistence that he speak to her before he would discuss the allowance, while not actually committing him to anything. Although if she had shown any enthusiasm, he would have had to offer formally, but the prospect of twenty thousand pounds would be powerful consolation.

Hathaway looked up from his work. "The dowry is not spoken of generally, Dalton. In fact, Winterton is thought to be rolled up, or close to it. A gamester, and one with neither sense nor luck."

"Hmm. So where did the twenty thousand come from?" Robin said thoughtfully. "The mother, probably. Settled on her and tied up so tight that Winterton could not get his hands on it. But he will miss the interest, that much is certain. What else did you find out about the lady in your listening at keyholes, Hathaway?"

The physician raised an amused eyebrow. "Nothing so low as a keyhole, I assure you. I merely mingle in the servants' hall or the stables or the local hostelry. It is astonishing how friendly villagers can be when plied with ale. Of Miss

Winterton herself and her sisters not a bad word is spoken. Paragons of virtue, every last one of them, and she has had suitors queueing for her hand for years, but she never looked at one of them until Mr Richard, and even then it was the third time of asking. Of the father, it is gaming. He goes to a discreet gaming house in Brinchester from time to time to lose a few hundred pounds. And he drinks, especially since the boy died. Drowned at sea on his first voyage as a midshipman."

"That *is* unfortunate," Robin said. "And there are no other sons?"

"None. But there is no entail on the estate, so the girls will not be thrown out to starve when the old man drinks himself to death."

"Assuming he does not gamble it all away," Robin said. "And what of my sainted brother? Please tell me you have heard some juicy gossip about him, Hathaway. A mistress or two, perhaps? A string of bastards? Or let him at least not pay his tailor."

"I am sorry to report that the late Mr Richard Dalton was indeed a saint. The only story I can find about him is a thwarted romance several years ago."

"Oh, do tell, Thomas," Lady Westerlea said, with sudden interest. "I do love a *thwarted* romance. The unrequited lovesick are so amusing."

"There is little to tell. He fell in love with a Lady Harriet Something-or-Other, she looked down her titled nose at him, and that was the end of it."

"Lady Harriet... Hawthorn?" Robin hazarded, scratching around in his mind for all the Lady Harriets he might know. "Scribster? Marford?"

"Marford! That was it!"

"Gracious!" Lady Westerlea said. "No wonder she turned him down. She is the sister of the Marquess of Carrbridge, and very much an old maid. Not inclined for matrimony at all, I should have said. Poor Richard! There was no hope there. Did he offer for her?"

"Oh, yes! Repeatedly, by all accounts. Was head over ears, without question. Carried a torch for her for years. She is a friend of Miss Dalton's, and stays here almost every summer, but in recent years Mr Richard would absent himself when she visited. Miss Winterton was very much his second choice."

"Now, why would she turn him down twice, only to accept on the third try?" Robin said. "Very intriguing. I wonder how much affection there was in the case, for her to refuse him twice?"

"No woman would rush to marry Richard, without the barony," Lady Westerlea said, with a languid lift of one shoulder. "So very *rustic*. There was no doing anything with him. A little town bronze would have improved him beyond all recognition."

"He is beyond all earthly improvement now, poor fellow," Robin said sombrely.

Only a few more days remained of their visit to the wilds of Brinshire, and already Robin's thoughts were turning to the return journey and the forthcoming season in London. He was in the library one day, inspecting the list of arrivals in town in the latest copy of the *Morning Post* to reach the provinces, when Miss Winterton was shown in. He had known her only for a few weeks, but he saw at once that her usual mask-like composure had been replaced by a state of great agitation.

"Miss Winterton, what a pleasure," he said politely, as he made his bow. "I trust you are well?"

"Oh… Mr Dalton, I…" She licked her lips, and looked around in a distracted way. "I have a problem."

"Whatever is the matter?" he said, crossing the room to her side in a few strides.

"I must talk to you!" she cried. "I… I do not know what to do. There is no one else I can turn to! Mr Dalton, I think… that is, I… oh, where to begin?"

"Come, now, do not distress yourself." He took her hand. "Tell me everything."

"I… " She heaved a deep breath, then went on in a rush, "Before he died, Richard…" Her hand came to her mouth, and for a moment she closed her eyes, unable to speak. He watched her in an agony of impatience. Another breath, then she continued more composedly. "Richard and I… we… oh, Mr Dalton, I believe I am with child, and I hoped… I thought perhaps, since you were so obliging as to… I thought you might marry me. Oh, I am so sorry! It is unforgivable in me. Pray forget I mentioned it."

To his own surprise, and without the least inward struggle, his life changed for ever.

"Of course I will marry you," he said calmly.

She burst into tears.

6: The Road To London

He led her gently to a chair near the fire, wondering at his own composure. If her suspicions were proved correct, then his future was now settled irrevocably, and he was not at all sure what he felt about it. Only moments before, he had been certain that he did not want to marry the girl at all, but now he actually felt quite calm about it. How very odd.

But the most urgent necessity was to find out if her fears were true. And if they were — well, he would smile and marry her and remind himself of the twenty thousand pounds.

"Sit here, Miss Winterton. Do you have a handkerchief? Good, good. Dry your eyes while I fetch you a brandy."

"I am so sorry," she said again, but already her tears were under control.

He shifted a footstool nearer so that he could sit at her feet. "Here, drink this. Do you have a firm hold of the glass? Good girl. And another mouthful. There, you will feel better directly."

"You are not shocked," she said, as he lifted the glass from her gloved hands.

He smiled at her naivety. "These things happen. Now, let us get this bonnet off..." He tugged at the ribbons and untied them. Then he expertly unbuttoned her gloves and peeled them off her hands, and began to chafe them. "You are frozen. There — do you feel a little better now?"

She nodded. "Thank you, sir. You are very good." He had never heard her so subdued.

"The first question must be — how certain are you of your condition?" he said.

She considered it thoughtfully. He liked that about her, that she never rushed to an ill-considered answer. "I am not at all certain. You will think me very foolish, I daresay, but the possibility had not occurred to me. If my mama were alive—"

"Of course," he said. "Young ladies are kept in ignorance of such matters until they marry, so it is not surprising if they are ill-informed about the details. Have you consulted a physician? Or a midwife?"

She shook her head. "I did not think to do so. Besides..."

"You do not wish anyone to know. I understand," he said quickly. Yes, the fewer people who knew the better. Have you told anyone at all?"

"No one, not even my sisters."

"Your maid may suspect, perhaps?"

"I have no maid of my own."

"Good. But it might be sensible to seek the advice of a physician. It may be that you are mistaken, and a physician would be able to set your mind at rest." And his, of course.

"My mother's personal physician is very skilled in the ways of women, and very discreet also. You may have every confidence in his judgement. My mother will have to know, in that case, for you will be seeing her own doctor, but no one else, I promise."

"You will not tell your father?"

"I see no need," he said. "It is a matter for the two of us only, and if I do not object to the situation, then no one else has any right to."

"And you do not object?" she said wonderingly.

He smiled in what he hoped was a reassuring way. "If it is indeed the case that you are with child, then it is a family problem, so it is for the family to resolve it, and that pleasure falls to me. Who better to protect my brother's betrothed and his child?"

"Thank you," she said again, but the sadness in her eyes tore at his heart. She had made one mistake in the expectation of marriage, yet the consequences could have been disastrous.

There was no point in delay, so he took her at once to his mother's sitting room, where Dr Hathaway could usually be found. It was the work of moments to explain the situation to him, and the doctor led Miss Winterton into the bedroom to conduct his examination.

"So the sainted Richard is not such a saint after all," Lady Westerlea said, with a brittle laugh. "And now you must throw the mantle of respectability over his cast-off wife and his almost-bastard."

"It is of no consequence," Robin said, sitting in the chair that Hathaway had vacated and stretching out his legs. He was unaccountably resentful at the talk of mantles of respectability, but he did not want his mother to suppose that he wished for the match. "It will save me the bother of dutifully bedding her. I am already provided with an heir." He was aware of a ripple of disappointment at the thought. Rosamund was very beautiful. Very enticing. Very *desirable.* But there was relief, too. It was better so. "Besides, I am relieved of the tedium of courtship. One wife is much like another."

It would also save him from the humiliation of rejection, or, worse, the embarrassment of falling in love. No man could maintain his dignity when he was abjectly prostrating himself before a woman, any woman. This way, he remained in control and his wife remained subservient and meek, and suitably grateful.

"You are too, too generous, Robin dear. Why did she not accept you when you offered for her?"

He hesitated, not quite wanting to admit that he had not, in fact, offered for her, only talked in a roundabout way of marriage. "She did not realise her situation then. One has to admire her honesty. She could have simpered at me and said she had changed her mind, without mentioning the little surprise she carries, and I might have found out later and hated her for ever. But this way..."

"This way she stitches you up completely. Has it occurred to you that it might not be Richard's bastard she carries?"

"Rosamund has honesty engraved on her very bones," he said sharply. "If she says it is Richard's, then it is so." Now why did he feel so defensive about her?

"Oh, so it is *'Rosamund'* now, is it? Very cosy."

"She is to be my wife," he said coldly. "Could you manage just a shred of respect?"

"Pfft," she said, with a lift of one shoulder. "I shall respect her twenty thousand pounds, you may be sure." Then, fretfully, "I wish they would hurry. I need Thomas. My head is aching abominably."

When Hathaway brought Miss Winterton back into the room, her eyes bashfully lowered, the physician said, "I can neither confirm nor deny it, Dalton. It is too soon for me to form a decided opinion. However, everything the lady says is consistent with the suggestion of a child. She has all the common signs."

"Very well, then," Robin said rising briskly to his feet. "This afternoon I shall inform my father of the happy news that Miss Winterton has accepted my offer of marriage. Tomorrow, Rosamund, I shall call on your father. At what time does he rise?"

"Not before noon, usually."

"Hmm. Then I shall go first to Brinchester to see the bishop and obtain a common licence, so that we need not wait for the banns to be read. I shall see your father on my return. And the parson, I suppose. The day after, we shall be married. And two days after that, we depart for London."

She raised her eyebrows. "So soon! I had not thought…"

"It must be so, unfortunately," he said. "Mother and I have unbreakable obligations, and must be back in London very soon to begin the process of making my cousin fit for her entry into society. No delay may be entertained without compromising her debut. It is all arranged."

"And you wish me to come to London with you?" Rosamund said quietly.

"Of course." He hesitated, not liking to be so blunt, but perhaps it was as well. "It will occasion comment if you are not with your husband, at least at first. Also, as your state becomes more obvious, there will be all sorts of perfectly natural questions from your friends which might make you uncomfortable. You will be better away from the society of those who know you well."

"I understand, sir."

She was so subdued — he hated to see her so crestfallen. "Let us go back to the library, where we are expected to be," he said.

"Very well, sir."

But by the time they had regained the library, Barnaby was already looking for Rosamund to tell her that the carriage was at the door, and there was no time for further conversation. He would have liked a few minutes in private with her, to reassure her that all would be well, and perhaps lift her spirits a little. Still, he supposed, if he were to be cynical, that they had the rest of their lives to talk in private, should they wish to.

Once she had gone and he was left alone, Robin tried to divine his own feelings on the matter. He ought to be shocked, he supposed, not to mention angry and martyred. He ought to be depressed at the prospect of spending a lifetime with this chit of a country girl. And his first child, possibly his first son and the heir to a barony, would not even be his.

And yet somehow he was not at all displeased. He would have a beautiful wife, who, when properly dressed, would be the toast of the *ton*, he would have a child without the least exertion and he would have twenty thousand pounds. He caught sight of himself in a mirror, and moved nearer to make a minute adjustment to his cravat.

"Well, my fine fellow," he said softly. "You are soon to be a very wealthy man. I congratulate you!"

He laughed, and went to find his father.

~~~~~

The marriage took place almost before the good people of Brinshire were aware of its possibility, and if the hasty match occasioned a certain amount of curiosity, the newly married couple were already on their way to London, and unable to hear it.

Rosamund watched the counties roll past the windows of the carriage each day. Brinshire, Staffordshire, Worcestershire, Warwickshire and now Oxfordshire. Towns, villages, inns, churches, pastures and woods passing in succession, each one much like another, and yet each unique in its own way. Robin had grown tired of her constant questions about their journey, and at their first stop in a town, he had dashed out to buy her a guide book. Whenever she looked across the carriage at him now, he was watching her with an amused expression on his face, and each time they entered a town, no matter how small and nondescript, he would say, "Well, Mrs Dalton? Is there a church tower of especial note? A rood screen of unusual magnificence? A medieval grain house? Or did Good Queen Bess sleep somewhere hereabouts?"

Mrs Dalton. She had almost grown accustomed to the thought that she would be Mrs Dalton, and then had been obliged to set aside the idea. And now, here she was, Mrs Dalton after all.

She could not quite decide whether she was pleased about it. No, that was foolish, of course she was pleased. Relieved, at least. Given the circumstances, how could she not be? Robin had rescued her from ruin, despite his own aversion to the match, and for that she must always be deeply grateful. She would try her very best to be a good wife to him, and not let him down. If only she were not required to go to London and participate in the season! He moved in such high circles, always talking of the duke of this and the countess of that. How could she ever hope to mingle with such people?

He had begun to educate her for her new role. "Tell me about the Duke of Purbeck," he would say.

"The present duke is the... um, fourth. Family name, Wareham. Family seat, Belsingham in Devonshire— no, Dorsetshire. The heir is the Marquess of Holme."

"Very good. The Duke of Camberley?"

"Oh dear. The fifth, I think. Or is it the sixth? The Marquess of Ramsey is the heir. I remember that because my brother had a tutor called Mr Ramsey once." And that brought back so many unhappy memories that she was almost overcome. "I beg your pardon," she whispered. "There is so much to learn."

"You are doing very well," he said kindly. "All this will mean more to you when you meet these people in person, and I shall be with you to help, after all."

He was very patient with her, and never reproached her, even though she was not an apt pupil. Yet how much better it would have been if he had married someone from his own sphere who already knew all these people.

Their journey to London was slow. Lady Westerlea was a poor traveller, so they proceeded at a leisurely pace, stopping often. Rosamund shared her mother-in-law's luxurious carriage with her ladyship and Mr Hathaway, the physician, as well as her husband. The luggage wagon behind them also conveyed Miss Horrocks, her ladyship's maid, Brast, Robin's valet, and Mr Simkins, her ladyship's secretary. The harassed Mr Simkins had written ahead to arrange accommodation at the best inns, but his mistress took not the slightest notice of his efforts, stopping wherever her whims decreed. As a result, the poor man had to contrive fresh lodgings each night for the whole party, including coachmen, postilions, footmen and two maids whose sole function was to attend to her ladyship's needs. Heaven forbid that she should be served by common inn servants.

Rosamund had no maid with her, since the maid she had engaged for her marriage to Richard had found another position.

"It is of no consequence," Robin had said. "Mama has already suggested someone for you in London, and while we are travelling, one of the inn servants will help you to dress and Horrocks will finish you off."

Finishing her off involved primping her hair into an elaborate style, adding more jewellery than Rosamund thought necessary and removing the small fichu she wore for modesty in so public a place. But on the second night, she waited in vain for Horrocks to appear. A gentle tap at the door sounded.

"May I come in?" Robin's voice.

"Of course."

"Mother is having one of her dithery days, so if you wait for Horrocks you will very likely miss dinner altogether. May I help out?"

"To dress my hair?" she said in surprise.

"I love arranging hair," he said simply. "I practise on my cousins when I have the chance, but it is a great disappointment to me that I never had a sister. May I?"

She was too surprised to refuse, but then she recalled that he was so fastidious over his own attire that he was probably well qualified to assist with hers. She was already seated before the looking glass, and he laid his hands on her shoulders and inspected her reflection.

"Hmm. What ornaments do you have for your hair?"

"The box over there holds everything of that nature."

He rummaged around, and produced a handful of jewelled combs and several necklaces. "Do you have any ribbons to match the gown?"

"In the larger box in the corner. The second row of drawers, the third from the left."

"Ah. Excellent. You are very organised. Now, let me see what I may contrive."

His fingers were surprisingly deft. He quickly plaited and coiled, securing the hair with combs, then weaving a ribbon about the crown so that the ends fell down her back amidst two long ringlets. A few soft curls framed her face. He swiftly chose a simple necklace, and fastened it around her neck.

"There — do you like that?"

She turned her head back and forth to admire his handiwork. It was simple, but looked surprisingly stylish. "I do — thank you!"

"You are lucky to have hair that curls naturally. You will see many women in London with very short hair, and such styles would suit you admirably, but I suspect the fashion will not last much longer. You might be better advised to keep it long for the moment."

"Thank you, sir. I am grateful for your interest in my appearance, for I shall not know how to go on in London."

"If you will put yourself entirely into my hands, I will make you into — well, whatever you want to be," he said with simple pride. "If you wish to be a leader of fashion, I can do that, but if, as I suspect, you had rather be elegant, I know exactly how to achieve it."

"Are *you* elegant?" she said before she could stop herself. "Or a leader of fashion?"

"The well-dressed gentleman should aspire to be both," he said gravely, but with a twinkle in his eye. "I suspect at present you think me a fribble, Mrs Dalton, but when you have had the experience of a season in London, you may see me differently. I must hope so, anyway. It is my ambition to hear you tell me, with sincerity, that I look splendidly attired."

She had no idea what to make of his words, but his tone was amused, not censorious and she went down to dinner not at all displeased with him. Mr Hathaway dashed in late, gulped down a random selection of food, and then disappeared in haste, muttering about her ladyship.

"I am sorry your mother is ill," Rosamund said. "What is it that ails her, exactly?"

Robin smiled. "Her nerves. She hates the uncertainty of travel, and it makes her fretful. Once we reach town she will be better."

"The travel would be less uncertain if Lady Westerlea would keep to Mr Simkins' proposed stops," Rosamund said tartly. "He has arranged everything for her comfort, yet she throws over his plans at every turn and herself introduces uncertainty."

With a laugh, Robin said, "That would be a logical conclusion to you or me. For myself, I value order and good regulation above almost all else, and you are a tidy person also. Only with effective organisation, such that every action is determined in advance and every article has its proper place, is to be found true peace of mind. Just as you can lay your hand on a certain ribbon without the least difficulty, so I am able to locate the exact pin or fob I require. My mother, however, is of a different nature. She is driven by her fears. She fears that Mr Simkins' choice of inn may not be suitable, so she passes it by and then finds herself obliged to stay in one even less suitable. She fears that the carriage will break down so she will only allow the coachman to proceed at the pace of a slug, whereupon she fears that she will not reach her destination and will be stranded upon the road at nightfall. She is beset by the dangers wrought by her over-zealous imagination. Poor Mother!"

Rosamund was surprised by his tolerance of his mother's foibles. He was neither impatient with her whims nor short-tempered with her fretfulness. He was far more easy-going and good-natured than she had supposed, and when they sat at table he was excellent company. She was so much in charity with him, that she ventured to say,

"What exactly is a fribble, sir?"

That made him laugh. "A man who clothes himself with frills and flounces and jewels like a woman. A fop or a coxcomb, on the other hand, is one who dresses to be the focus of all eyes, and will wear the most outlandish styles to achieve that aim. A pink is a man at the height of fashion, and a tulip is one who merely dresses well. Whereas a beau..." He sighed. "Ah, Mrs Dalton, to be a beau like Mr Brummell would be a fine thing indeed, for a beau is an arbiter of fashion, one who leads rather than follows, a person of influence in society. Such a man buys only the very best clothes, and wears them with the greatest attention to detail but without ostentation or undue show. He is admired and respected, his views listened to, his presence sought everywhere. I should dearly love to be described as a beau."

"Then I hope you get your wish," she said. "For myself, however, I had sooner be described as kind or good or generous. I like to be correctly attired for the occasion, but I do not wish to turn heads when I walk into a room."

He smiled. "Then you had better avoid leaving your own house, my dear, for your looks are such that you cannot avoid such an outcome." She blushed and, with a laugh, he reached across the table and took her hand. "How delightfully you blush! You are so composed that it is a great triumph to bring colour to your cheeks. You are charming, Rosamund, quite charming."

But he did not find her charming enough to share her bed. That night, as on every night since her marriage, she slept alone.

7: Carloway House

Rosamund had no idea what to make of her husband. She had indeed thought him a fribble, and still did, but he was also an intelligent man, well-educated and well-read, with a surprisingly kind heart. He had told her in plain terms of his distaste for the prospect of marrying her, yet when she had thrown herself upon his mercy, he had agreed to it immediately, and had made not one reproach since then. Far from regretting his decision, he seemed to be going out of way to convince her that he held her in real affection. *'Quite charming'*, he had said, and she could detect no insincerity in his manner. If he were playing her false, it was beyond her skill to find it out. She had the unsettling feeling at the back of her mind that she was being manipulated into compliance, but he would soon find that there was no need. She would play the smiling wife for his friends to the best of her ability. She had wanted this marriage as little as he, but now that it was accomplished she would not repine.

For all his fashionable clothes and grand society manners, he was good company, whether alone with her or with others. He had dined at Woodside the night before their marriage, the first time he had met her sisters. They had stared at him in wide-eyed silence, unable to comprehend why Rosamund had changed her mind after swearing that she could never marry such a man. And she had meant it, too, but naturally she could never explain the circumstances to any of her sisters. They were maidens still, and need not know the dark secrets of intimacy between a man and a woman. She had said glibly, "It seemed a sensible move — to unite the two families, as I had hoped to do with Richard." She knew they did not believe her. Probably they assumed she was determined to have her title, and were disgusted with her. They would be even more disgusted if they knew the truth.

Her father had been so cross that evening. It was not like him to be unwelcoming towards a guest, but so it was. He was abrupt almost to the point of rudeness with Robin, and not at all his usual affable self. She supposed it had to do with the disagreeable business of settlements, which had so discomposed him before.

Robin, by contrast, had been all civility, taking pains to know each of the sisters and complimenting the food with apparent sincerity. He had spent a full hour closeted away with Papa and the port decanter after the sisters had withdrawn, and after that Papa had seemed more at ease. Still, it was an odd sort of evening altogether, one where only Robin had appeared quite comfortable. It was the sign of a gentleman to be at ease in any company, Rosamund reminded herself, whenever she was inclined to magnify Robin's faults. Whatever else he might be, he was truly the gentleman.

So her thoughts ran during the long hours in the carriage, when conversation flagged.

Carloway House was larger than she had envisaged. Since it accommodated only Robin and his mother, she had imagined a modest town house of six or eight rooms, but this imposing double-fronted edifice looked like a mansion to her. A butler and two footmen emerged to receive them, and in the hall a row of six or seven maids stood in a line, bobbing curtsies. Robin showed Rosamund to her bedroom, a huge, high-ceilinged room overlooking the street.

"Mother dislikes the noise at the front of the house, so you and I must tolerate the calls of the lamplighters and the rattle of the coal merchants' carts," he said with a wry smile.

"I do not mind that," she said. "I used to have an owl seated on the tree outside my room at Woodside, and no lamplighter could be noisier, I assure you."

He laughed at that. "Your dressing room is here, and my room is through that door. Ah, here is Marie, who is to be your maid. I recommend the blue muslin with the white flowers on it for Mrs Dalton this afternoon, Marie, and the blue bandeau in her hair. The green figured silk with the overtunic will do very well for this evening. When you are changed, Mrs Dalton, I will show you around."

With a bow, he went through the connecting door to his own room.

Marie giggled, not bothering to curtsy to him as he left. She was an unlikely sort of maid, for she wore a very pretty muslin gown and little lace cap with dark curls peeping from beneath it, and had not the least degree of servility. She would have looked perfectly at home drinking tea with the matrons of Brinshire. However, she efficiently tracked down the blue muslin and bandeau, and dressed Rosamund very deftly, although with much French muttering over the buttons.

Robin was waiting on the landing for Rosamund when she emerged. He had changed too, exchanging his buckskins and top boots for pantaloons and hessians, and adding a different waistcoat and coat. He now looked much more the sophisticated town dweller.

He pointed out his mother's bedroom, and Mr Hathaway's next door — "For convenience if Mother is unwell during the night," Robin said — and the two rooms that Lady Westerlea's sister and her daughter would occupy when they arrived.

"They will be here the day after tomorrow, as planned," Robin said. "We expected to reach home tomorrow, but we made such good time that we are here a day early. It is often so, when Mother panics and presses onwards. We arrived a day early on our northern journey, too. It is excellent news for you, for I have sent word to Madame Aubert, and if she can arrange it, she will be here tomorrow and you will have her undivided attention to plan your new wardrobe."

"Is my old wardrobe so inadequate?" she said.

She was speaking in jest, but he answered her seriously. "It was well enough for Brinshire, Mrs Dalton, but it will not do for London, not for the sort of occasions you will be attending."

They had descended the stairs by now, and he showed her the drawing room and music room, the saloon and morning room, pointing out with pride the objects of interest in each room, many of which he had chosen himself. Dutifully she admired the fireplaces, chandeliers, painted ceilings and wallpapers. Even a particular chair was given special mention, although she could not say honestly whether it pleased her or not. Art of such a nature was beyond the reach of her aesthetic sensibilities. So long as a chair was fit to sit on, that was all she asked of it. On the floor below was the dining room, cloakroom, card room and Robin's own study. It was the first room where he made no comment on the furnishings or decoration. Instead, he led her into the room and watched her as she looked about, an expectant expression on his face.

It was the first glimpse of the nature of the man beneath the surface, so Rosamund looked around with interest. Books, lots of books, ordered by size. A pair of pictures, of the modern type. A row of snuff jars on the mantel, arranged with perfect symmetry. Two wing chairs either side of the fire. A large desk under the window, and alongside it a table with a peculiar brass contraption.

"What is this?"

"A microscope. For examining things too small to be seen with the eye."

"What sort of things?"

"Insects, a drop of water, a leaf…"

"A leaf may be seen with the eye," she said, puzzled.

"Ah, but there is so much more to be seen through the microscope," he said eagerly. "The intricacy of the veins, the beautiful patterns of the cells, and the colour so vibrant and alive! It is nature at its most magnificent."

"It is usually said of nature that the most magnificent instances are also the largest — the great oak in the forest, the mountains and rivers, the sky in its splendour at sunset."

"Those are good examples," he said, "but it is in the detail that cannot even be observed by the eye alone that we see the hand of God in all its glory, the minute detail that we would not ordinarily know of. It is the most wondrous thing!" His face was alight with enthusiasm and she had never seen him so animated. "I wish I could show you at once, but all my prepared slides are boxed up in the cellar for safe keeping. But you may see something of the amazing creatures that may be observed through the microscope, if you look at this book." He pulled a heavy volume from a shelf, flicked through the pages and then opened out a folded drawing. "There! Is that not the most fascinating being?"

"It is very beautiful. What is it?"

"Why, it is a louse."

"A *louse!*" She burst out laughing. "How may so troublesome a creature be so beautiful? But you are quite right — the drawing is fascinating, and I should be glad to know more on the subject."

He beamed happily at her. "It will be my pleasure to share my findings with you. Do you like my study — my sanctuary?"

"Very much." Impulsively she added, "Are you glad to be home?"

"Of course," he said simply. "London is so vibrant and busy, it makes me feel alive. But then... I daresay you feel that way about the country."

"I cannot say, having never lived anywhere else. Certainly the country appeals to me, with its peacefulness and beauty, and the freedom from the demands of everyday life. One may walk through the woods and leave all one's cares behind. Perhaps I shall like London too, when I am used to it, but there are so many strangers here. It is the familiar faces around one who make life enjoyable, it seems to me."

He looked at her quizzically, as if unsure how to take her words, but he made no comment.

When Rosamund went to dress for dinner, she found Marie still busy unpacking. The green evening dress that Robin had suggested lay on the bed awaiting her. For a brief moment she was tempted to ask for a different one, but there was no point in antagonising both her husband and her new maid on a whim. It was her own gown, after all, bought for her marriage, and perfectly suitable for an evening at home. Had she been asked, she might well have chosen it herself. It was only Robin's rather domineering manner that rankled. Even though he had termed it a suggestion, he would have been surprised to be countered in any way. Well, he knew more of London fashions than she did, so she would not cross him unless she felt it imperative.

"Not sure what *zat* is," Marie said, pointing to the bed. "Was in wiz ze stockings. Is not ze proper place, I feel."

The broken rein of Richard's, which Rosamund had almost forgotten about. She picked it up, and examined the broken ends, partly smooth, as if cut, and partly torn. How foolish to keep it! There was nothing suspicious about Richard's death, surely, and the only person who benefited by it had not even been there—

She stopped, inhaling sharply. But Robin *had* been there! He and his mother had arrived a day early, had he not told her so himself? He had been there, and could easily have walked down to the stables... But that was ridiculous. The immaculately attired Mr Robin Dalton, who probably never went near a stable in his life, wandering unnoticed about the stables at Westerlea, finding precisely the rein that Richard would use the following day and cutting it half through? No, it was impossible.

Besides, she thought uneasily, he was her husband now, and not at all the self-absorbed man of fashion she had initially supposed him to be. Had he not been kindness itself to her? Yet the thought would intrude, that he now had his brother's place in the world and also his brother's wife—

No, that was a nonsensical idea. She stuffed the strips of leather hastily into her workbag and set it out of her mind.

The first evening at home after several days of travel should have been a restful one. At Woodside, the tradition was that any member of the household arriving home after a journey was treated to all their favourite foods at dinner, and allowed to choose what activities were to be pursued afterwards. Rosamund had no expectation of such special treatment at Carloway House, but with Lady Westerlea already fast asleep in her bed, dosed with laudanum, and only herself, Robin and Mr Hathaway at table, it should have been a pleasant enough evening.

It was not to be, for Robin was set on continuing to train her for her entry into London society. Half the dishes on the table were awkward to eat in one way or another, chosen so that she might learn how to tackle them. She was expected to converse sensibly on whatever topic Robin chose, without hesitation, even while wrestling with her braised larks and quails' eggs. When she gave an answer he deemed correct, he instantly moved on to some other subject. There was no respite after dinner, for Mr Hathaway went upstairs to attend her ladyship and Robin followed Rosamund through to the drawing room almost at once. She was required to play on the pianoforte three pieces that he had selected to test her capabilities. When she had muddled through those, he brought out the cards and played piquet with her, until her head was spinning with elder and younger hands, parties and talons, tierces and quatorzes. She was almost dizzy with exhaustion by the end of the evening, her head throbbing.

Never had she been so glad to retire to her room. Marie undressed her and readied her for bed, all the while relating amusing little anecdotes in broken French, which Rosamund hardly had the energy to smile at. But as soon as Marie had gone, she crept out of bed again and sat cross-legged on the floor in front of the dying fire. At such a time, she missed her sisters so fiercely it was almost a physical pain. After a difficult day, they would gather in one or other of the bedrooms, the others with their hair in curling papers, and discuss the events of the day together. No matter how trying her problems were, Annabelle, Lucy, Margaret and Fanny could always restore her equanimity, as she could theirs. The simple routines and familiar practices were immeasurably comforting.

But now she was alone. Her mother, that bulwark against the travails of the world, was in her grave. Her sisters were far away. Her father, even were he present, would be staring into a bottle. Her only protector was Mr Robin Dalton, a man she barely knew and did not even like very much. No, that was not true. She had begun by despising him quite thoroughly, but there was a kindness in him at times that she could not but respond to. He was still unpredictable, however, and she did not feel she could depend upon him.

As she sat watching the last flickering flames, she could hear his voice in the adjoining bedroom, as he talked to his valet before bed. Only a connecting door separated her from her husband. One night, she supposed, he would come through that door to claim her. Well, she could not object to that. It was part of the bargain of marriage — he gave her his name, his position in society, his wealth, and she gave him... whatever he asked of her. Even the right to choose her gowns for her, if that was of importance to him. But she shivered. Truly she was alone.

Eventually the fire died down and she grew cold, so she crept back to bed. Her thoughts were racing around inside her head so much that it was a long, long time before she fell asleep, and even then her repose was far from tranquil. She slept fitfully, jerking awake often with the thought in her head that there was somewhere she had to be, and she was late. Sometimes there would be a cart rumbling past in the street, the noise unfamiliar enough to wake her, but sometimes there was nothing but stillness and she could not understand why she had woken.

And then she dreamt. She was in a dark place, a cellar perhaps. Someone was there with her, for she could hear breathing close by. Heavy breathing, right beside her. She could not move. It was imperative that she get away, but her legs would not work, and she was caught, like a fly in a web. He was there, speaking to her, his voice harsh, but the words were unintelligible.

She was lying down, and he was close, so close she could hear his rapid breathing in her ear, hear him panting. It was Richard. Speaking her name...

"Rosamund... Rosamund..."

No! Terror rose up, choked her throat, brought her to blind panic.

"No, please no!"

"Rosamund!" The tone was urgent. He grabbed her arms, he was shaking her...

"Get away from me!" she screamed.

Then she opened her eyes. His face was an inch from hers... *"Go away!"*

It was Robin.

He jumped back as if stung, hands raised in apology. "Sorry! So, so sorry! You were dreaming, and I—" He had backed right across the room by now, setting his candle guttering on her bedside cabinet. "I beg your pardon. Are you... quite well? May I send for Marie?"

"Marie?" Her maid, she remembered. "Oh... no. Thank you. It was... just a dream. Gone now."

"You look very pale. Some brandy?" His own face was ashen, his eyes wide with dismay. He wore only his nightgown and nightcap, she saw. He must have heard her cry out and come rushing through to help.

She raised herself to a sitting position, rubbing her face, trying to erase the hateful memory of the dream. And other memories. She was still shaking violently. "I... I am all right. I think. Just a dream. Thank you."

"And... and there is nothing... you require?"

"No... thank you."

"Then I will leave you."

And with that he turned and stumbled back to his own room, one hand against the wall as if he feared to fall. The door closed behind him.

She was alone.

8: Lessons

Robin was shaking as he regained his room. He had left his candle in Rosamund's room, so the only light was from the last embers of the fire. He felt his way back to bed, and then sat on the edge rocking slightly. It was not anger he felt, so much as dismay. He had always known that she despised him, for her feelings could not be disguised when she had first met him and looked him up and down with such cold disdain. Nor had she married him from choice. Since then, she had hidden her feelings rather well, and was unfailingly polite to him, without the least hint of rancour. He had taken the greatest care to be gentle with her, and not rush into anything.

But he had hoped — oh, how he had hoped! — that her dislike was beginning to fade away, and that in time she might even grow fond of him. But her words... *'Get away from me! Go away!'* And the look in her eyes! What was it... fear? More than fear, terror. Hatred, perhaps. Yes, hatred, and she had been looking straight at him as she cried out, so it could not have been the residue of the dream.

Lord have mercy, how could she hate him so much? Had she been so deep in love with Richard that any substitute was unworthy in her eyes? Or was it more personal — perhaps it was Robin himself, his very character, that she abhorred. And what could he possibly do to improve his standing in her eyes?

Then he wondered why it mattered to him what she thought.

Eventually he dozed a little, before his valet woke him bringing his hot water. With a sigh, he rose and began his morning toilet. Usually the routine of washing, shaving, dressing and arranging his hair soothed him. The rasp of the shaving knife, the smooth feel of clean linen against his skin, the delicate matter of the neckcloth, for the complicated arrangements he preferred took all his artistry to achieve, the choosing of a fob and finally the coat... it took a long time, but the result was, in his eyes, a perfectly judged balance of fashion and elegance. The disordered man who stumbled, bleary-eyed, from his bed was transformed by painstaking degrees into a gentleman of substance. The result was not showy but it declared him a man of exquisite taste.

Or so he liked to think, and it rankled that his own wife thought his appearance less than admirable. He was still rattled by her rejection of him when, finally satisfied with his appearance, he descended to the dining room for breakfast. She was alone in the room, sitting with her head down, crumbling bread with surprising intensity.

"Good morning, Mrs Dalton," he said, bowing to her rather stiffly. She looked pale, he thought, but she was wearing the morning gown he had suggested for her, which was perhaps a good sign.

She looked back at him gravely. "Good morning. Crest is just fetching the chocolate."

"No Hathaway this morning?"

"He has been and gone already." She looked down at her plate of crumbled bread, then up at him as if she wished to speak. But then she looked down again.

"No more bad dreams, I trust?" he said, in what he hoped was an affable manner. But how difficult it was to talk to her normally, when his last memory was of her anguished face screaming, *"Go away!"*

She shook her head, then suddenly looked up and leant forward, her expression intent. "Pray forgive me!" she whispered. "It was dreadfully rude of me to speak so to you, when you were only trying to help. I did not mean... it was not... it was the dream, nothing more."

He thought her distress was genuine, but he no longer trusted himself to know what she was thinking. He wanted to take her hand, to smile, to reassure her that he understood, but he was not sure that he did. In London society, he understood the nuances of conversation perfectly, and could distinguish between the words spoken and the intent very well. With his own wife, from a very different background, he could not begin to understand her mind.

"It is of no consequence," he said eventually. Then, because he had no idea what else to say to her, he said, "Madame Aubert will be here very soon to begin measuring you for your new gowns. That will take some time. We shall need to see all your good jewellery, to ensure the colours are properly matched."

"I have no good jewellery," she said, with a smile. "Just a few trinkets, and I believe you have seen all of them already."

"Hmm. I understood there was jewellery... from your mother?"

"Papa could not find any of Mama's pieces. I suppose they must have been sold."

"It is of no consequence. If there is time after you have seen Madame, I suggest you practise on the pianoforte. Your performance is tolerable, but you need to work at it more diligently before performing before a London audience."

"Yes, sir," she said, eyes lowered again. "Do you think I will be required to perform in public very often? In Brinshire, I seldom played upon the pianoforte, except reels and such like for impromptu dancing. For a musical evening, I am more competent upon the harp. But if you wish me to improve my skills upon the pianoforte, I shall do so, of course. I should not wish to disgrace you."

She seemed so earnest, like a child talking about her lessons, that his lips quirked into a little smile. "If you prefer the harp, I shall buy you one."

Her eyes widened in surprise. "Thank you, sir. You are very kind."

~~~~~

Rosamund could not make her husband out. At breakfast, his manner had been cold and distant, and who could blame him, after she had been so unspeakably rude to him? Yet as soon as she had mentioned the harp, he had offered to buy one for her. He could be the epitome of kindness, at times. Then she fretted that he might buy the wrong size. Should she tell him what to buy? Or suggest that she should choose it? Her own harp at home had come from London originally, so she knew where to find another such. But he was so overbearing that he might take such suggestions badly. It was so awkward.

Madame Aubert had already arrived by the time Rosamund had finished breakfast, so there was no opportunity to catch her breath and prepare herself for the onslaught. For onslaught it was. Madame herself and three helpers, together with Marie and Robin, all crowded into Rosamund's bedroom, examining every item of clothing she possessed and Rosamund herself, all the while chattering away in French, not a language Rosamund had ever learnt. She was competent in Italian, but by the time Mama had decided to teach her daughters French, Rosamund was practically out and unwilling to start afresh. It was unsettling, she found, to be measured in twenty different directions, and then to be the subject of detailed discussion amongst the others, without having the least idea what they were saying about her. Madame would point to one or another part of Rosamund's body, and then they would jabber away, nodding or shaking heads in the most disconcerting manner.

It was not until Madame said something directly to Rosamund herself, and they all looked expectantly at her, awaiting her answer, that she said composedly, "I beg your pardon, but I cannot understand you. My French is very poor."

Marie burst out laughing, but Robin frowned. "You should have said so earlier, rather than letting us go rattling on."

"I beg your pardon," she said, uncomfortably, hanging her head. "It had not occurred to me that I was expected to have an opinion."

"Of course you are expected to have an opinion," he said sharply. "No one will impose anything upon you against your will. Really, Mrs Dalton, you must think me a very domineering sort of husband if you imagine otherwise."

Since she did indeed think him domineering, she had no answer to this, except to apologise again.

"Madame, we say nozzing bad about you," Madame Aubert said, with a hearty chuckle. "Only zat ze legs are too fat for ze beauty."

Robin winced. "Not fat! Well-built, perhaps. All that horse-riding does not make for slender legs."

"Ah, but my fat legs help me to dance all night," Rosamund said, spinning round so that her skirt swirled out. "See? Dancing is almost as much fun as riding."

Marie giggled, but Robin's expression did not lighten.

"Ah, *mais oui,* ze English women like to ride," Madame Aubert said. "Such a pity! But Madame has ze most beautiful... ah, *le sein?*"

"Bosoms," said Marie. "Beautiful bosoms. Display ze bosoms, and no one looks at ze legs."

Rosamund laughed. "I thank you for the compliment, but I do not wish to display my bosoms."

There was a collective intake of breath. "Madame! It is ze fashion!"

She looked helplessly at Robin. "Must I?"

To her infinite relief, he immediately said, "By no means, if you dislike the idea." The Frenchwomen all groaned at this capitulation, but Robin gave a wintry smile. "You French all think that *la mode* is all that matters, but here in England, *style* is of greater significance. One must be fashionable too, naturally, but it is more important to have *presence*. Mrs Dalton has, as you have so correctly observed, an excellent figure, and her deportment is likewise striking when she remembers it." Rosamund immediately straightened her back and lifted her chin. "Yes, that is much better," he said, with a sudden warm smile that made her glow a little inside. "You see, Madame? Mrs Dalton does not need to wear a gown that draws attention to itself. It should be subtle, enhancing the beauty that is already there, so that when she passes by, strangers will turn their heads to follow her, and enquire of their companions, *'Who is that very handsome woman?'* Do you see, Madame?"

"*Mais oui!* Subtle, *oui*! Enhancing, *oui*! Zis I can do, Monsieur."

"If you wish for an ideal upon which to base your efforts, Madame, I suggest the Marchioness of Carrbridge, whose style is always of the utmost elegance, without straying too far from current fashions, yet never extreme."

"Ooh, ze Marchioness, *oui*. Now zere is a handsome woman indeed. I understand you perfectly, Monsieur. Subtle, and not so much ze bosoms. Now, we look at ze *morceaux de tissu*. Madame Dalton, put on ze cream silk over zere, *s'il vous plait*. Let me see how you look before ze hand of Madame Aubert transforms you."

Rosamund and Marie went into the dressing room and she changed into the silk evening gown. It was one of her newest gowns, chosen for her marriage, and she was rather pleased with it. She had two different over-dresses to wear with it, or for a less formal occasion it could be worn on its own.

When she returned to the bedroom, Madame had strewn fabric samples onto every available surface, so that the room looked as if a whirlwind had swept through it.

"Ah..." Madame said, and then the scrutiny began all over again, back view, front, view, side view and, naturally, the bosoms. Rosamund was amused rather than offended by the very frank commentary. If it pleased her husband to dress her up for London society, with no expense spared, then she had no intention of interfering with his plans. How glorious it would be to have a wardrobe stuffed full of beautiful gowns and pelisses and frivolous little bonnets, of the sort that she had never been able to afford before. And as many silk stockings as she wanted. She sighed with pleasure, and moved back and forth between the dressing room and the bedroom, putting on one outfit after another for Madame's practised eye to examine. Only when the dinner gong sounded did she realise that she had spent an entire day dressing and undressing.

And then another evening under her husband's tutelage, the only difference being that Lady Westerlea was sufficiently recovered to join them for dinner. She talked languidly to Mr Hathaway while Robin instructed Rosamund. Over the first course, they covered the latest news from the Peninsula, small pox, taxation and a small part of the Wars of the Roses.

During the second course, it was the West Indies and sugar, the health of the Prime Minister, more on taxation, and the construction of Norman castles. By the time the dessert was set out, they were back to lists of dukes.

"I shall find you a copy of Debrett's," Robin said. "Then you may begin on the marquesses. Tell me about the Duke of Dunmorton."

"Really, Robin dear," his mother said mildly. "Your wife is not some schoolroom chit, to be taught her lessons."

"Oh, but it is all most interesting, Lady Westerlea," Rosamund said.

"Interesting? Small pox?"

"Very interesting," she said firmly, with perfect truth. "My only regret is that I am not an apt pupil. It must be frustrating for Mr Dalton to repeat everything so many times. The Duke of Dunmorton is the eighth of that line, he lives at Castle Morton in Northumberland and his heir is the Marquess of Darrowstone. The family name is... Wyndham. No... Wilbraham? No, I have forgotten."

"Winfell. What about the Duke of Portland?"

Lady Westerlea rolled her eyes in disbelief. "Shall we leave the gentlemen, Rosamund? All this catechising is making my head ache." She dozed in the drawing room for half an hour until the gentlemen rejoined them, whereupon she felt sufficiently restored to play whist for two hours.

Rosamund was exhausted by the time she reached her bed that night. She had the dream again, and woke to find

Robin in her room once more. This time, however, he stayed beside the door, candle in hand, calling her name.

"Sorry..." she murmured, still fuddled from sleep, dragging herself upright. "So sorry. Dream..."

"Is there anything I may get for you?" he said.

"No... thank you. I am so sorry to have woken you."

"It is of no consequence. Shall I light a candle for you?"

She shook her head, and with a clipped, "Good night, then," he departed.

~~~~~

Lady Westerlea's sister arrived as expected the following day, a woman of careworn appearance and pinched features. She was the widow of a clergyman, and had no desire to re-enter society herself, but wished her daughter to have the chance of making a better match than she had herself. Since she had a dowry of six thousand pounds, it was to be supposed that she would be successful.

Or so Robin had previously thought. His first sight of his cousin, Miss Charity Carrington, was not encouraging. She had, as Madame would say *'ze slender legs'*, but the rest of her was just as slender, and Madame would certainly lament the lack of bosoms. Still, a good dressmaker and the right stays would correct or hide a multitude of deficiencies. The teeth were more of a problem, giving the poor girl a striking resemblance to a rabbit.

"Oh dear," Lady Westerlea said, as Charity made her first curtsy to her aunt.

"I know," Mrs Carrington said. "She is no oil painting, is she? But the sweetest nature imaginable."

"It is quite all right, Aunt," Charity said. "No one expects me to catch a husband, but I should so like not to be laughed at. If you can make me look respectable, and allow me to dance at Almack's, that is all I ask."

"You will be able to do something with her, Felicity, I am sure of it," Mrs Carrington said. "You are so well-dressed yourself, you will know just how to turn her out."

"Oh, Robin will take care of that," Lady Westerlea said airily, waving a scented handkerchief in his direction.

"Robin? A *man?*" Mrs Carrington said. "You would allow a man to determine poor Charity's wardrobe?" She looked at Robin properly for the first time, taking in the shining boots, the skin-tight inexpressibles, the perfectly aligned waistcoat and coat, and the neckcloth, arranged today in the very difficult Mathematical style. "Ah," she said.

He did his best, no one could say he did not, but Charity was not easy material to mould. Not like Rosamund, who could be transformed into a society lady by the mere addition of a stylish gown and a feather or two in her hair. Poor Charity never looked anything but the dab of a girl that she was. But Robin was determined to make something of her, so he persevered. Madame Aubert came to work her magic, a frighteningly expensive woman came to cut and dress her hair, a music teacher and dancing master gave lessons every day, and he continued his wide-ranging discussions with Rosamund in the hope that Charity would also benefit by it.

Rosamund needed no instruction from the dancing master. Country dances, the cotillion and even the quadrille she danced effortlessly, and with considerable grace.

"Do you include the waltz in your repertoire?" Robin said to her.

"Oh, no, it is too fashionable for Brinshire. I saw it danced once at the Brinchester Assembly Rooms, to great consternation on all sides. The population was so scandalised that it has never been attempted there since."

He laughed. "Well, you need not participate if you find it too scandalous, and you are not alone in that opinion, but it is much danced now at private balls. Should you like to try it?"

"I am not sure... It is a very intimate dance, is it not?"

"It is, and I do not consider it proper for an unmarried lady, but you may dance it with your husband without the least impropriety."

"With you? Oh, I should like that!" she said with the utmost simplicity.

So Mrs Carrington played a waltz tune, and Robin taught his wife the steps. She blushed a little, and he was somewhat discomposed himself. He had danced the waltz many times before and, after the first time, had not thought greatly about the intimacy of it. Now, with his own wife, he found himself all too aware of the warmth of her body beside his, of his arm resting about her waist, of her eyes fixed on his, of her *nearness*. To his astonishment, he wanted nothing more than to crush her into his arms and kiss her, and it took every ounce of self-control he possessed not to do so.

"You are an excellent dancer," he said rather breathlessly when the dance ended.

"I was about to say the same to you," she said. "That was most enjoyable. Thank you!"

Her smile was so warm and her eyes so bright that the urge to kiss her did not diminish in the slightest, and it was only Charity saying, "Goodness! That was— My goodness!" in shocked tones that recalled him to a sense of his surroundings. He bowed to Rosamund, and she curtsied demurely, and they moved smoothly on to another country dance, but the incident had unsettled him, and the expression on her face haunted him for some time.

Was it possible that she liked him after all? He had never looked for love in this strange marriage, but a certain fondness would be agreeable and would lead to a harmonious home life. Yes, that was all he hoped for — harmony, and a degree of placid acceptance of each other. He tried not to wonder why he felt this tremendous desire to kiss those entrancing red lips, but for the first time he felt pleasure in his marriage that had nothing at all to do with the increase in his wealth.

This happy state lasted for precisely three days, when Brast arrived with his shaving water and the ominous words, "Mrs Dalton sends word that she would be pleased if you could attend her in her bedchamber at your earliest convenience, sir."

"Is she ill, Brast?"

"I couldn't say, sir."

After a moment's thought, Robin realised he could not allow his wife to wait for the two hours it would take him to dress properly. If the matter was urgent, as such a summons implied, then he must go to her at once, however distasteful it might be to present himself to her not even shaved. He shrugged on a robe and knocked tentatively on the connecting door.

"Come in." Her voice was so low he could barely hear it.

She was already dressed, which made him feel even more shabby to be standing before her in his nightgown and bare feet. Her hair was loose, however, falling forwards over her face. She sat in the window seat, knees drawn up to her chest, her face half hidden, not looking at him.

"You wished to see me?"

"Yes. I thought you should know at once that I am no longer with child."

Still she did not look at him, and now he understood — it was guilt. She had drawn him into this marriage because of her condition, and now that need was swept away. Although her calmness was odd — surely she should be upset? That suggested a worse thought, so that anger burned through him.

"Were you ever with child?" he said coldly. Her head swivelled round to stare at him. "Or was it just a ploy to trap me into marrying you?"

"How dare you!" She was on her feet, fists clenched, cheeks flushed, eyes sparkling with rage. "How *dare* you! Do you really think I would stoop to such a low trick, just to marry a *popinjay* like you? You are insulting, sir! And if only we had waited, it would not have been necessary. I am just as trapped as you are, let me remind you."

His anger had evaporated as suddenly as it had arrived. He realised at once that she was right, and her condition could not possibly have been a pretence, for had she not always despised him? No, she must have been forced into marriage, just as he was. And all for nothing, now.

Yet as she stood before him, her chest heaving, he had never seen her look so beautiful. He was breathless with admiration, although he could never, ever admit to such a thing. And yet, she thought him a popinjay. A parrot. His restrained elegance contrasted with a gaudy and exotic bird. The insult ran too deep for him to make any reply. He turned and stalked back to his own room.

9: A Rout At Lady Alreagh's

As soon as Robin had gone, Rosamund hurled herself onto her bed and burst into tears. She had thought he might be angry, but to suppose that she would resort to trickery—! It was beyond insult.

But the reasonable part of her mind soon reasserted itself. He had been taken by surprise, and saw only her composure. He had not seen how distraught she had been hours before when she had summoned Dr Hathaway to confirm her suspicions of what was happening. He had not seen the tears she had shed, the endless pacing about her room, her near-hysteria at the cruel workings of fate. She had now had several hours to come to terms with the changed situation, which had been sprung on Robin with no warning. Of course he was angry and suspicious.

So after a while, she dried her tears, ordered a breakfast tray to be brought to her, and prepared to face her future with equanimity. The first task must be to reach a rapport with Robin, and not let the disagreement fester. So when she had eaten, she sent for Marie to dress her hair and make her ready to face the world, or at least her husband. Her enquiries as to his whereabouts led her to his study on the ground floor. She paused outside the door, took a deep breath and then knocked.

"Enter."

She went in. He was bent over his brass contraption in the corner, but he looked up in surprise as she came in. She was in plenty of time to see the cold mask of contempt fall across his face as he recognised his visitor.

"Mrs Dalton?"

She curtsied sedately. "Mr Dalton, I am come to apologise for my intemperate language earlier. It was unpardonable, but I trust you will overlook it this once, given the circumstances."

He stared at her with cold dislike.

Quietly, she went on, "This is the moment when you accept my apology and proffer your own."

"For what do you imagine I have to apologise?"

"You suggested I ensnared you into marriage. The idea was so offensive to me that I was prompted to reply in like manner."

When he said nothing, she rushed on, "Pray forgive me, for I did not mean it."

"But you did," he said flatly. "Do you know the expression *'in vino veritas'*? It means *'in wine, there is truth'*. Well, there is also truth in words spoken in anger. I thank you for your honesty, madam, for I now know your true opinion of me."

"Then your words to me must also bear the same charge," she cried, "for were they not spoken in anger also? Did you not accuse me of trapping you into marriage?"

"Then we are both equally insulted," he said, his eyes hard.

She huffed an impatient breath. "This is not helpful. We were both angry, we both said things we did not mean, as everyone does at such times. Mr Dalton — Robin — let us indeed be honest. If we had met in the usual way, neither of us would have been drawn to the other. I am too provincial and ill-educated for a man like you, and you are too fashionable for me."

"A popinjay," he sneered.

"So I thought at first. I have seen another who dresses in like style, a Mr Arthur Cromwell, and I held the same opinion of him, for I knew as little of his character as I knew of yours, at first. And perhaps he is nothing more than a fine dresser, a man of vanity and nothing else. But of you, I have learnt differently. Since we have been thrown together in this unexpected way, I have come to see that beneath that elaborately tied cravat there is a great deal more depth to you than I had supposed. Right from the start I understood it, for when your brother left me in difficulties, you stepped in with the greatest generosity of spirit, for which I shall always be deeply grateful. Since then, you have been kind to me in a thousand ways, and you must not suppose me insensitive to your good nature. What has happened has happened, and cannot be undone, so we are stuck with each other, but I very much wish to be a good wife to you. We are bound to quarrel occasionally, for that is a part of human nature, but so is forgiveness and reconciliation. You are too amiable, I am sure, to resent my over-hasty words, which I now deeply regret."

He looked at her with an unreadable expression on his face. Oh, if only she could understand him! He was such a complicated man, an odd mixture of odious pride and generosity, and could veer from one to the other as the wind changed. Some men were simple, and could be kept sweet by the regular appearance on the table of a good dinner and a wife who smiled often, but Robin was not such a man. She had not the key to his moods, but perhaps openness could increase her standing in his eyes.

When he said nothing, she tried a different tack. "Do you wish me to go home?"

"This is your home." He sounded bewildered.

"I meant to Brinshire. To Holly Lodge."

"Of course not. That would attract comment. You must stay and do the season, however much you dislike the idea."

So hostile. But he must not think her unwilling. "I do not dislike the idea, if it is what you wish, and I confess to a great desire to meet some of these people I have been learning about." That brought a twitch of the lips that might possibly be called a smile, if one were feeling generous. "Robin... since we cannot escape from each other, may we not at least be friends?"

"Friends..." he said in a tone that sounded puzzled, almost as if he did not know what she meant. Did he have any friends? No one had called on him yet. Lady Westerlea had received calls, but Robin, so far as she knew, had not. A few cards left, but nothing more. How curious.

She waited. Now that she had said her piece, it was for him to determine the way forward. Would he be cold, distant Robin, or would he smile at her in that way he had that made her feel warm inside?

He licked his lips, and rubbed one hand against his coat nervously. "I... I have retrieved some of my prepared samples for the microscope from the cellar. I have a fritillary... a butterfly ready for viewing. It is very beautiful. Would you like to see it?"

It sounded like an olive branch, and she accepted it as such. "Thank you, I should love to."

He led her to the microscope and showed her how to look through it. She cried out in delight. "Oh, the pattern! It is extraordinary!"

He gave a pleased laugh. "It is, is it not? And the colours... so vivid. Although they fade a little with time."

"But what are these giant metal skewers?"

"Pins. The butterfly is pinned so that the wings stay in position."

"Poor creature!" she said. "Held for ever in one place, and never free to fly away again."

"It is quite dead," he said gently. "And the pins make it easy to observe the detail of the wings. Even in death, this fritillary is helping us to understand the mysteries of the world around us. Is that not a glorious way to die, for the advancement of science?"

"I prefer living butterflies," she said. "Is it not better to observe the creature as it lives and moves, on the tree or flower, basking in the warmth of the sun, rather than cold and dead? An hour walking through the woods of Brinshire shows me more mysteries of the world than your microscope could reveal in a month."

"There is value in both," he said, smiling.

But all she could think of was that she herself was pinned just as securely as the butterfly, by her own unwanted marriage.

~~~~~

Rosamund's first social event was a rout at Lady Alreagh's. There would be cards, food and drink, but no dancing, Robin told her. He chose her gown and the manner of arranging her hair, as he did for Charity Carrington also. Lady Westerlea, whose role it was to chaperon Charity and introduce her to society, would be the only other member of their party.

She ought to have been nervous, but Rosamund was surprisingly calm. Her first appearance in London society should have reduced her to a quivering jelly, and even Robin was jumpy, but Rosamund had attended enough dinners and balls and card parties not to be unduly anxious. It would be a larger and grander event than any she had yet seen, and some of the other guests had the power to destroy her socially, or so Robin told her. But somehow she was unworried. She had her husband to steer her through the shoals of the *ton* and guide her away from the rocks, and she had heard enough now of some of society's leaders that she was fuelled by a powerful curiosity to meet these people and judge them for herself. And besides all that, she had a splendid new gown to wear, not showing too much of her bosoms, with new shoes and stockings and gloves of such wondrous softness that she took them out of their drawer each night just to feel them. Her hair had been cut just a little, and arranged in a flattering new style, and only that evening Robin had presented her with an exquisite set of sapphires to wear — necklace, ear drops and a bracelet. She felt like a princess.

"You look very well, Mrs Dalton," Robin had said to her in tones of surprise, waiting in the hall as she descended the stairs.

She smiled and dipped him a curtsy. "If so, it is entirely your doing, Mr Dalton."

He bowed to acknowledge the compliment, but he smiled a little too, and it pleased her to see him in a good mood at the start of the evening.

Charity arrived in the hall not long afterwards, and Rosamund was forced to acknowledge that she looked remarkably improved. With her hair short and feathery around her brow, the teeth were hardly noticeable, and as for her lack of bosoms, it was astonishing what might be achieved with a good set of stays and some extra frills around the gown.

Even Robin smiled. "Ah, cousin Charity... excellent."

She missed her step, and almost tripped over the hem of her gown. "Oops!" she said, with a giggle, and Robin's sigh of despair was almost audible. But his smile never faltered.

Lady Westerlea drifted down the stairs a full twenty minutes after the appointed hour, when the horses had already been walked three times around the square to keep them warm, but Robin made no reproach. They entered the carriage, he tapped on the roof with his cane and the equipage lurched into motion. Ten minutes... that was all the time it took them to reach Lady Alreagh's house, and Rosamund was quite sure they could have walked it quicker, for the last few hundred yards were a crawl in a snaking queue of similar vehicles. However, one did not walk to an evening engagement in London, even when the destination was only two streets away. They arrived, they were decanted into the street under the stares of the local population, they walked the few paces to the foot of the steps, they ascended and entered the house.

Charity's eyes were round at the brilliance of so many candles, and the number of smartly-liveried footmen to receive their cloaks, and Robin's hat and cane. Rosamund was less impressed. The house was no bigger than Carloway House, and she was accustomed to the grandeur of country mansions, with echoing entrance halls three stories high. This narrow little passageway was uncomfortably crowded, and the room they were directed into was no better. So much noise! There must have been a hundred people crammed into the space, and all of them talking at once. Robin handed over their cards to the announcer, who banged his staff on the floor.

"Lady Westerlea, Mr and Mrs Robin Dalton, Miss Carrington," he boomed.

They inched forward into the press of people, made their courtesies to a harassed Lady Alreagh, a round dumpling of a woman in a puce turban with several huge feathers stuck into it, and moved on into the throng. Lady Westerlea was immediately claimed by an acquaintance, and disappeared into the crowds, talking animatedly. It was astonishing how a woman who spent her life stretched out on a chaise longue, too fatigued to stir, could summon so much energy for a social event. She left Charity behind, and Rosamund suspected Lady Westerlea had, for the moment, forgotten the girl's existence.

A line of footmen held trays of drinks, but Robin steered them past and scanned the room carefully. After a moment, he said, "We will go this way, I think." He set off in a different direction from his mother. Rosamund now saw that the tightly-packed throng was, in fact, composed of numerous groups, small and large, chattering away excitedly to each other. Robin nodded to several people as he passed by, and a number bowed or curtsied in return, and several glanced at Rosamund and Charity with interest, but Robin moved purposefully onwards, through an arch into a second room, and then into a third, each a little less crowded than the one before. But the fourth room was full to overflowing.

"Lady Alreagh keeps the best drinks as far away as possible," Robin said. "Cheaper for her, and most guests never notice. But for those of us in on the secret..." He waved a languid hand around the room, to encompass the horde of gentlemen, and a few ladies, already supplied with glasses of champagne or wine, and clearly enjoying the evening a great deal.

Robin obtained three glasses of champagne from an impassive footman. "There! Drink, Mrs Dalton, Cousin Charity, in celebration of your first London season. It seems likely to be a good one, for there is more of a crush here than I expected. There are quite a few people back in town already."

"Thank goodness!" Charity said. "A drink at last." She drank half the glass at a single swallow and emitted a loud hiccup. "Oops!"

"Dalton! What a squeeze, eh?" A hearty young man of almost thirty flung an arm around Robin in a brotherly way. Robin raised one eyebrow a minute amount, but his smile never faltered.

"Ramsey. How are you?"

Ah, yes, Ramsey. The Marquess of Ramsey, heir to the Duke of Camberley. She had the dukes off by heart now.

"Oh, tolerable, tolerable. And who is this lovely lady with the lustrous eyes?" His gaze may have begun at Rosamund's eyes, but it soon strayed downwards and there it lingered.

"This is my wife, Ramsey," Robin said, without rancour. Rosamund could not be sure, but she thought she detected amusement, as if it pleased him to have other men ogle his wife.

"Well, you lucky dog! Will you not present me?"

"What is your opinion?" Robin said to Rosamund. "Do you wish for an acquaintance with such a dreadful rattle?"

"Why certainly, for rattles produce the most amusing flummery," she said archly, and he threw her a sharp glance, as if wondering whether her words had more than one meaning.

But Lord Ramsey laughed long and loud. "Why, I like a lady with wit as well as beauty. Come, come, man, introduce me!"

"Mrs Dalton, cousin, may I present the Marquess of Ramsey. Ramsey, Mrs Dalton. And this is my cousin, Miss Carrington."

Lord Ramsey glanced briefly at Charity, then lost interest.

"And which county do you call home, Mrs Dalton?"

"She is from Brinshire," said a voice at their elbow, as a very tall lady wearing an almost diaphanous gown materialised from the crowds. "Heavens, Ramsey, do you not read the papers? Dalton, my condolences on the death of your brother, although it is a fortunate circumstance for you, I daresay. And congratulations on consoling the bereaved fiancée so successfully." She threw a considering glance at Rosamund.

"Bella..." Lord Ramsey said uncertainly.

"Oh, I do not blame her," the tall lady said. "One does not marry the heir to a barony for love, so when one heir is taken from you, why not move on to the next in line? Very sensible, I call it. A most effective little scheme."

Robin's arm twitched convulsively, but his smile never faltered.

"Really, Bella!" Ramsey said in some alarm. "Mrs Dalton, I must apologise—"

"Do not distress yourself, Lord Ramsey," Rosamund said calmly. "There was bound to be gossip amongst those ignorant of the true circumstances."

Bella tittered, ignoring her. "I wish you joy of your bride, Dalton. An excellent match, by all accounts, and the evidence is there for all to see." She threw an amused glance at Rosamund, then turned back to Robin. "Such magnificent sapphires!"

"They are pretty, are they not?" Rosamund said pleasantly, not liking to be ignored.

"Pretty? Oh yes, very pretty indeed. But you can afford it now, eh, Dalton?"

And with another snigger, she strolled away, her hips swaying in a way that Rosamund had no difficulty recognising. London society was not, after all, so very different from that to be found in the provinces.

10: Mistress Of The House

"Well, *that* was rude!" Charity said stoutly.

Ramsey laughed, and looked at Charity properly for the first time.

"Indeed it was, Miss Carrington. I apologise for my friend."

"Is she your friend? I should be ashamed to have a friend who talked so."

"You are perfectly right. I shall drop the acquaintance immediately."

"Well done!" she said approvingly, and Ramsey bowed.

Robin frowned. Was the marquess flirting with his cousin? He could not possibly be serious, for Bella Dryton was his mistress and he could hardly cut her publicly while sharing her bed. And why would he flirt with Charity? Ramsey was the heir to a dukedom, and one of the most eligible bachelors in England. He habitually kept well away from unmarried women who might entice him into matrimony. No doubt he would marry some dreary duke's daughter some day, but certainly not Miss Charity Carrington of Nowhere-in-Particular.

"What nonsense, Ramsey," Robin said tersely. "Cousin, Lord Ramsey is teasing you, I fear. One does not abandon an old friend on a whim."

"Why ever not?" Ramsey said. "Bella is only a viscountess, after all, and on a question of good manners, one must always obey the strictures of a lady."

He smiled at Charity with such warmth that Robin was immediately on his guard. He had seen that look in Ramsey's eyes before. It was absolutely necessary to distract him. "I do believe Lindsay is trying to attract your attention."

"Where? Ah, so he is." Ramsey looked conscious, as if realising that he was flirting outrageously with a debutante, and turned his attention back to Rosamund. "You will excuse me, Mrs Dalton, I trust? We shall meet again very soon, I am sure, and if you are to attend the Fallons' ball, keep the first two for me. Good evening to you, Miss Carrington. A pleasure to make your acquaintance." So saying, he dashed off to greet a young man with a violently coloured waistcoat.

"Should I do so?" Rosamund said, smiling up at Robin in a way that made him rather flustered. "Keep the first two dances for Lord Ramsey, that is?"

He wanted to give a very brusque answer, but it would not do. One must not show that one cared in the least who one's wife danced with. Naturally, he did not care in the slightest, but somehow the very idea of her wasting her smiles on Ramsey stuck in his throat and made him choke.

And after the dance, what then? No, Ramsey should not have her!

His answer needed to be casual, as if it mattered not at all. Still, it took all Robin social skills to answer with tolerable equanimity, "Regrettably, you cannot, for you are already engaged."

"Am I? To whom am I engaged?"

"To me, of course! As if I would allow your first appearance in a ballroom to be alongside that loose fish!"

"But he is a duke's son," she murmured. "Perfectly unexceptionable. And it is hardly my first appearance in a ballroom, Mr Dalton, only the first in London."

"If you think the Brinchester Assembly Rooms bear any comparison with—" he began crossly, but then stopped with a spike of alarm. She was drawing him into unacceptably disordered behaviour. Calm... he must be calm and controlled. Deep breath. Calm... controlled. Another breath. Perfect control at all times. "Let us walk through the rooms and see who has arrived lately," he said in more moderate tones.

"By all means," she said equably. "I shall abandon my champagne here, if you have no objection. If this is the best, I am glad I did not try the inferior stuff."

He laughed, suddenly quite in charity with her. "Quite right. Lady Alreagh is a trifle tight-fisted, but do not tell anyone that I said so."

"My lips are sealed," she whispered, and that made him laugh again.

As they moved away from the abandoned champagne glass, from the corner of his eye he noticed Charity scoop it up to replace her empty glass, and made a note to keep a careful eye on his cousin. She was not quite the demure debutante he had expected, which was a good thing in many ways, but he did not want her getting bosky at her first outing.

Rosamund, however, needed no watching. Robin was rather impressed with his wife. He had assumed her calm composure would melt away when faced with the full glory of the *ton*, but she was not in the least disconcerted. They strolled arm in arm through two rooms, Charity trailing behind them, and this time Robin stopped to speak to this group or that, and to introduce Rosamund and Charity. They received a pleasing degree of respect, and only one or two made reference to Rosamund's former betrothal to Robin's brother. He had expected the gossip to be in full flow. The notice of Richard's betrothal, followed by his death and, very swiftly, by Robin's own marriage was bound to occasion comment, and it seemed that half the *ton* knew of Rosamund's dowry. That was Aunt Mary's doing, no doubt. She rarely came to town but she knew many of the famous society hostesses. He had no objection to that, for it provided a simple explanation for the hasty wedding, and increased the respect due to him. Yes, he was a man of independent wealth now. He was somebody to be taken notice of.

By the time they had reached the first room again, Robin's ruffled feelings had been so far soothed that he was in charity with the world, and had no fault to find with the company or his wife or himself. And there was his reward, the one person above all others he had hoped to see.

"Over there, in the centre of that large group," he whispered to Rosamund. "What do you think of him?"

"The man in black, being fawned over so excessively? He is handsome enough, I daresay."

"I do not mean his looks. What is your opinion of his manner of dress?"

"Ah. It is very plain and neat, so I cannot fault him there, but black is such a dull colour for evening, is it not? I like a blue coat, like yours, or a wine colour, as Lord Ramsey chose. A black coat makes me want to offer my condolences. But it is a beautifully cut coat, and fits him to perfection, and the neckcloth is a work of art."

Robin sighed. "A perfect Oriental. I have never mastered it, not to my satisfaction. He will always have the better of me there."

"I am looking at the celebrated Mr Brummell, I assume?" she said, smiling up at him with a teasing look in her eyes. "Your hero."

Before he could reply, a female voice squeaked, "Rosamund? Is it you? I daresay you do not remember me, do you?"

Robin stiffened with shock. The Marchioness of Carrbridge! How could Rosamund possibly know her, and, more to the point, why had she never talked about her?

"Of course I do, Lady Carrbridge. Mrs Blank's little dancing school for young ladies, on Rush Lane, Brinchester, which lasted... oh, a whole summer, almost."

"I know, I know," Lady Carrbridge said. "I was so disappointed, for we so seldom left the house except for church, but even Papa agreed it was unexceptionable. But I saw in the newspaper that you are not Miss Winterton any longer. Is this your husband? Will you introduce me? And to your friend?"

"It would be an honour. Lady Carrbridge, may I present my husband, Mr Robin Dalton, who is heir to Lord Westerlea of Brinshire. And this is his cousin, Miss Carrington of Suffolk. Mr Dalton, Miss Carrington, the Marchioness of Carrbridge."

He bowed low, Charity dropped into a deep curtsy, and the marchioness dipped a small curtsy in reply. "Mr Dalton, how sorry I was to hear about your elder brother. He was one of the first gentlemen to stand up with me at a ball, when I was but seventeen and terrified that I would be a wallflower, so as you may imagine I have the fondest memory of him. Although I seldom saw him after that. He was not a man who liked to dance, I think, but he was very gallant towards me."

"Richard was a man who took life very seriously," Robin said. "Dancing was a duty to him, not a pleasure, so he saved his ventures onto the dance floor for only the most beautiful and accomplished young ladies."

"Oh, a very pretty compliment," Lady Carrbridge said, laughing. "I thank you, sir. Your husband is charming, Rosamund. Shall we elbow our way into Mr Brummell's circle of admirers? I wish to remind him that he is invited to dine with us next week."

"He will not have forgotten, I am certain," Robin said, "but do not let us keep you from his entertaining company. We must admire the gentleman from afar, for I have not the honour of acquaintance with him."

"Then let me introduce you," she said. "Come, follow me."

And so it was that an evening that he had been so nervous about, and which had started inauspiciously with the snide remarks of Bella Dryton, had become an unforgettable high point in Robin's life. He quite forgave his wife for not mentioning her acquaintance with Lady Carrbridge, and gave no thought at all to Charity Carrington or Lord Ramsey.

~~~~~

Rosamund found herself enjoying the season far more than she might have expected. She did not like London very much, for it was dreadfully noisy and crowded and smelly, and she missed her rides and her long walks through the woods desperately, but attending a ball almost every night was thrilling. Some nights there were two or three different events requiring their presence, and then there were outings to the theatre or to Vauxhall Gardens. Most nights she danced until dawn, then slept until noon or even later. Then there might be shopping or visiting to fill in the hours before the next round of evening entertainments. There was something very restful about being a married woman and not having to worry so much about being demure, or weighing up possible suitors.

It was as well that she had met Lady Carrbridge, for Robin's friends were mainly single men of his own age, and his mother's friends were older women. But her very slight acquaintance with Lady Carrbridge had given her an opening into that lady's extensive family. Two of her sisters were in town, sensible women who moved in less lofty circles, but were also from Brinshire. It was very comfortable to have friends with whom to discuss mutual acquaintances. Lord Carrbridge and his brothers were rather more elevated personages, and eccentric, as noble families often were, but they too accepted Rosamund and her husband as part of their circle of friends, to Robin's great delight.

Rosamund was beginning to have a clearer picture of her husband now that the season was under way. He clung to the nobility and was inclined to be dismissive of anyone without a title. He always accompanied her when she called on Lady Carrbridge at Marford House, or when that lady or one of her sisters-in-law might be expected to call on Rosamund, but she went alone to visit Mrs Ambleside and Mrs Burford at their more modest rented house. Only a few commoners met with his approval, and those few headed by the incomparable Mr Brummell himself. His highest ambition was to be accepted into the Prince of Wales' set, and he was astonished to find that Rosamund thoroughly disapproved of His Royal Highness.

"He is the most dissolute and vulgar man imaginable," she said firmly. "And quite unprincipled."

"But very fashionable," Robin said mildly.

"Being fashionable is all very well, but one looks for more substance in one's friends," she said at once. "Morals, for instance, and restraint, and kindness, and generosity to those below them on the social scale."

Robin raised a surprised eyebrow, but made no attempt to argue the point. After a few moments, he said, "I could not afford to move in those circles anyway," and the subject was dropped.

Rosamund did not mind his odd quirks, for she was becoming comfortable with Robin now. He still had not come to her bedroom, but he treated her well, had bought her jewels and even a harp, although his first purchase had been too big for her to play and had had to go back. But he had laughed and taken her there to choose another, and encouraged her to practise every day.

He seemed pleased with her reception by the *ton*. It would be too much to say that she was a success, but she was acknowledged everywhere and invited to every event of note, and Charity was included in this happy state of affairs. She might not have Rosamund's beauty, but once she grew accustomed to society, she was discovered to have an open and engaging nature which won her many friends, and not a few suitors. There was no doubt that she would receive an offer of marriage or two before the end of the season, and Robin was generous enough to ascribe her success to Rosamund's influence.

She would almost say that she was happy. This was not the life she had chosen, far from it, and there was still the return to Brinshire to be undertaken, so that Robin might be trained for his future role as baron and landowner, but for the moment she was content. Even the dreadful nightmares, filled with Richard's implacable face, had faded away and troubled her no more.

One minor thorn in her side was her maid, Marie. As a maid, she could not be faulted, but there was an arrogance about her that Rosamund could not like. She dressed almost as fine as a lady, which was ridiculous in a maid. At first Rosamund had taken Marie with her when she had gone shopping to carry parcels, but twice when she had stopped to exchange greetings with someone, her acquaintance had asked to be introduced to Marie. It was embarrassing to confess that the smartly dressed young lady accompanying one was in fact a maid. Yet when she had suggested to Marie that she wear something more appropriate, Marie had simpered and said she rather liked her present clothes. After that, Rosamund had taken a footman as parcel-carrier, who at least could not be mistaken for her social equal.

Then there was the odd way Marie was regarded within the household. She seemed to give orders to the servants, and sometimes she had overheard them addressing her as *'Madam'*. It was all most unorthodox.

The final straw came when Rosamund was out in the carriage one day, and passed Marie in the street wearing one of Rosamund's own pelisses and its matching bonnet.

As soon as she returned home, she sent for Marie, pacing up and down the morning room in a fury as she waited. The maid arrived in the morning room wearing her own clothes again but with a kind of insolent sneer on her face.

"You wished to see me, Madam?"

"That is so. Marie, why did I see you on Huntly Street wearing my pelisse and bonnet?"

Marie tittered. "Did you, Madam? You were not supposed to see zat. It is very nice bonnet, no?"

Rosamund could hardly believe the girl's impudence. She was so shocked she could hardly speak. Her voice sounded harsh to her ears as she said, "You will pack your things and leave today. I shall write you a good reference, but I do not want to see you again."

"Oh, I zink not, Madam."

"I beg your pardon, but you are my maid and if I say you are to leave, then you leave." She took two steps forward, her hands clenched into fists, and for the first time uncertainty crossed Marie's face.

"Is not so simple. I find you anozer maid, but—"

"Get out! *Out!*"

With another titter, half defiance and half fear, Marie made to leave. Defiance won the day, for at the door, she turned and looked triumphantly back at Rosamund. "If you want to know how it is, ask her ladyship. She engaged me."

And with those words, she departed.

Rosamund set off at once to follow her advice, stamping up the stairs in a pelter. Whatever Marie's position in the household, surely Lady Westerlea would understand that such misconduct could not be ignored. Such insolence in a servant was intolerable. Lady Westerlea would be taking her afternoon nap, but it was imperative to speak to her at once, so that Marie might be turned off without delay.

She rapped sharply on Lady Westerlea's bedroom door. There was some scuffling from inside, and creaking that sounded like the bed. Then, softly, but quite distinctly, the snick of a door closing.

"Enter," came Lady Westerlea's languid voice. "Oh, it is you. What is it? Is the house on fire?"

She was in bed, in her chemise, her hair loose about her shoulders, the blankets disordered on one side as if someone had just left them. Rosamund was too angry to care. So what if she had a lover? That was between her and her husband.

"I want Marie turned off," she said.

"What? Marie? What has the silly woman done now?"

"She has been parading herself about town in my clothes, if you please. And now she says I may not discharge her, for it was you who engaged her. So *you* must turn her off, and today, if you please, for I will not have her in the house a moment longer. It is insupportable!"

To her bewilderment, Lady Westerlea laughed. "Such outrage! Of course I will not turn her off. What an idea!"

Rosamund gaped at her.

"Oh, you little provincial!" Lady Westerlea said. "Do you not realise who Marie is?"

Numbly, Rosamund shook her head.

"Why, she is Robin's mistress, of course."

"His *mistress?*"

"Of course. How could you not know? Now do get out. I am very tired."

Rosamund stumbled out of the room. Her own room was nearby, so she retreated there, too stunned to know what to do. He had a *mistress?* No wonder he had been in no hurry to visit her bedroom. But to allow the woman to live under the same roof as his mother and his wife, to act as her lady's maid, that most intimate of positions... Words failed her. She was shaking, her legs too weak to support her, and she almost fell onto the bed.

For some minutes she sat, struggling to calm her breathing, to stop herself from quaking like a leaf in the wind. It was the insult that she could not fathom. Robin was so particular about manners, was unfailingly polite to her... to everyone. He was so correct, and yet he saw fit to offer such an egregious affront to his wife's dignity. Did he laugh about it with his friends? *Oh, no, she has not the least idea! Thinks she is nothing but a servant. Is it not delicious? And so convenient...*

No, surely Robin would not abuse her so. Would he?

At least she knew now what she must do. If Marie were Robin's mistress, then it was for him to get rid of her. She was not going to suffer even one more night under the same roof as that woman. Her rage now was turned to icy determination. She leapt up from the bed and went downstairs. Robin, she discovered from the servants, was in his study. She knocked and strode straight in.

He was bent over his microscope. When she entered the room, he looked up, first in surprise, then with a pleased smile and finally, perhaps reading her furious expression, warily.

She did not wait for him to speak. "Is Marie your mistress?"

He stood, and she could almost see him casting about in his mind for an answer that would placate her.

"It is a simple enough question. Is she your mistress or not?"

Still he said nothing, licking his lips nervously.

"I have my answer, I suppose," she said coldly. "She leaves this house today."

"Wait a moment," he said, coming towards her. He had removed his coat so he wore only his waistcoat over his shirt. She had never seen him so informally dressed before. "Marie cannot leave."

"Today!" she hissed. "She leaves today, or else—"

"Or what?" he said, a jeering tone in his voice.

She had not thought about the consequences of her demand, but she did not hesitate. "Either she goes, or I do. Which is it to be?"

His eyebrows lowered. "Now you are being absurd."

"Absurd? To not want to share a house with my husband's *mistress*? Who is also my personal maid. Whose ingenious idea was *that*, I wonder? Yours? Hers? Or did you cook it up together?" She no longer cared what she was saying, her anger spilling over beyond her power to control it. "How amusing, to have the mistress waiting on the wife! Well, no more. Are you going to get rid of her, or do I go? I am sure there must be a hotel somewhere—"

"Stop it!" he cried, striding towards her so fast that she took a step backwards. "Stop this nonsense at once. Who are you to give me orders?"

"I am your *wife!*" she cried. "I am the one person above all others you should treat with respect, not insult."

"Oh, you want respect?" His face was an inch from hers, eyes narrowed to mere slits, his face red with anger. "Yes, you are very respectable *now*, now that I have married you. Where would you be if I had not?"

She slapped his face so hard his head spun sideways, the crack of her hand on his cheek echoing around the room. If she had thought him full of anger before, now he boiled over, grabbing her wrist so hard it hurt. She gasped in surprise, but she was still too fuelled with rage to be afraid of him.

She lifted her chin in defiance. "Are you going to hit *me* now? Go on, hit a woman, you coward!"

He grabbed her other wrist, and with an impatient cry she tried to pull away from him.

"Stop it!" he yelled.

Again she wrestled with him, but all she achieved was to back herself against the wall. "Let go of me!"

"Stop this," he cried, and hauled her wrists upwards so that her arms were above her head. There he held her, pinned to the wall just as surely as his butterflies were pinned when he looked at them through his microscope.

"Stop it, stop it, stop it!" he said. "Please…"

And to her utter astonishment, he leaned forward and kissed her.

11: Dinner For Two

Rosamund's experience of kissing was limited to just a few occasions with Richard. This kiss was nothing like those. The moment Robin's lips fell onto hers, pressing into her with frenzied ardour, she was caught in the spell. Even with so little familiarity of the art, she understood that Robin's kiss was driven by raw passion, and she could no more resist him than stop breathing. She felt his anger and frustration and desperation, but also need, and she could not deny him.

Nor did she want to. Her hunger matched his own, and she poured all her misery and grief and loneliness into that kiss. In that moment, in that place, she needed him just as ardently as he needed her. All the proprieties and restrictions of her life dropped away until there was nothing but Robin and his desperate kiss, two people bound together by something so powerful she could not break free of it. They kissed and kissed and kissed, warmth filling her until she felt as if she was on fire, glowing from head to foot. She wanted that kiss to last forever.

He was the one who pulled away first, jumping back as if stung, releasing his grip on her so abruptly that her arms dropped like lead. He held his hands up in front of him as if to ward her off. She had never seen him look so shocked, almost distraught. He stared at her, his eyes huge, taking great heaving breaths, saying nothing. Perhaps he was as incapable of speech as she was.

Then, without a word, he half ran for the door, as if he could not wait to get away from her.

Her legs gave way, and she slid down the wall to find herself sitting on the floor. In the silence of the room, her breath came in great rattling gasps that shook her from head to toe. What on earth had happened there? All restraint between them had vanished, all the surface veneer of politeness stripped away until all that remained was this incredible heat burning them up. She felt... she could not even describe what she was feeling. Her thoughts swirled around her head like a flock of starlings. If she were to be tossed into a room full of people, she doubted she could string words together to compose an intelligible sentence. If she tried to curtsy she would assuredly fall on her face.

What was the matter with her? She had been kissed before, but not like that. She had never experienced *anything* like that.

Somewhere in the house she heard voices, raised voices. A door slammed. At another time she would have been shocked to hear such sounds in this most restrained house, but now all she could think about was Robin and that kiss and wonder how she could manoeuvre him into a repeat performance. She pulled her knees up and rested her head there, eyes closed, savouring the astonishing waves of emotion washing through her. She, who had always been so calm, so practical, to be swept away in this hysterical manner, like a crazy woman.

Voices in the hall outside the study door, angry voices and quiet ones, and banging noises, as of heavy objects being moved. The angry voice was shrill, now, but the words were all in French. Then the front door creaking open. Another stream of invective, thumps and shuffling noises, the lower voices of the footmen. The front door closed. Footsteps receded and all was blissful silence once more.

She retreated back into her reverie, where there was nothing but Robin. Her Robin. She wondered if she were falling in love. How strange that would be! To start by despising a man so thoroughly and yet come to love him. He was such a coxcomb... and yet there was such a gentle heart beneath the stiff exterior. He had so many good qualities that she could respect — his kindness in marrying her, for one thing, and his devotion to his mother, who was not the easiest person in the world to get along with. Yet he never showed the least impatience with her whims and fancies.

It was true that he was not a countryman, not like Richard had been. Robin was at home in London, surrounded by the cream of society and its entertainments. He was not a man who could spend a whole day fishing or shooting or riding over muddy fields — how dreadful if the least speck of mud should soil his buckskins! He was not at all comfortable aback a horse. When she had mentioned to a dinner guest how much she missed riding each day, Robin had at once hired two hacks and himself accompanied her to Hyde Park each day. Neither of them had enjoyed it, she because she could not gallop without scandalising the *ton*, and he because he ended each outing smelling of horse and was obliged to bathe and change from head to toe afterwards. So they had given it up, and he had taken her driving in his curricle instead, which was very pleasant. He was an expert with the reins—

Reins. She had almost forgotten the broken rein from Richard's horse, the rein that had perhaps precipitated that fatal plunge. The rein that had snapped clean through… or been cut. And Robin had been there the day before the hunt. Robin was the one who benefited from Richard's death, and would now be Lord Westerlea one day, instead of his brother. And she was halfway to being in love with him! More than halfway, if she were truthful. And yet, surely he could not be responsible? He had so disliked the idea of being the heir! Although, perhaps that had merely been a ruse. Had he secretly envied his brother, perhaps for years, but then came the news that Richard was to marry, and so Robin surprised everyone by appearing for the wedding, with murder in mind. It made a horrible kind of sense. And yet, somehow, she could not believe it of her husband. No, it was impossible.

The door flew open, making her jump. It was only the housemaid, come to attend to the fire. She could not see Rosamund, half hidden by the door, so Rosamund closed her eyes again and ignored the sounds of vigorous sweeping and raking going on at the hearth. The afternoon sun was making the room warm, and she was half asleep when the maid, her work completed, turned back for the door, and gave a yelp of surprise.

"Oh, ma'am! I didn't see you there. Beg pardon." She bobbed a curtsy.

"It is quite all right, Betsy."

"Yes, ma'am."

She hovered for a moment, but it was not her place to enquire why her mistress was sitting on the floor, so she slowly backed out of the room and clicked the door shut behind her. Rosamund drifted away again.

A few minutes later the door opened again and this time it was Robin who entered. Even with her eyes closed, the scent of him was familiar enough to recognise. He said nothing, but she heard the chink of glass, and then liquid being poured.

"Rosamund?"

He was still without his coat, which made him look quite undressed. He seemed uncertain, like a boy.

In his hands were two brandy glasses. "Here... this will make you feel better." He sat on the floor near her and then gently pushed one glass along the floor until it was within her reach, as if not wishing to get any closer to her than necessary for the purpose. Then he slid himself backwards so that he was resting against a chaise longue, and sipped his own brandy.

She sat motionless, watching him. He sat with one leg bent under him, the other upright so that his chin almost rested on the knee. He had such long legs. His face was pale, and he looked exhausted, all the spirit knocked out of him. He seemed young and tentative and defenceless, nothing like the arrogant society man.

"I looked everywhere for you," he said at length, not looking at her, his voice a mere thread. "When I could not find you, I was afraid that you had... gone. Left the house. It never occurred to me that you might have stayed exactly where you were." Then, pleadingly, "Will you not drink? Just a little. Please."

Her practical nature reasserted itself. Brandy might indeed make her feel better, or at least more like her normal self. Carefully she picked up the glass and drank. Her hands were hardly shaking at all. She drank, and put the glass down again. She supposed she ought to say something... apologise for her earlier behaviour... something... But her tongue refused to shape the words. She sat, as still as a statue and as incapable of motion, the warmth of his kiss still swirling through her veins.

He cleared his throat, almost as inarticulate as she. He drank again and then set the glass down. "Marie has gone," he said, gazing intently into his glass as he swirled the brandy about. "Not quietly, but she has gone."

"I heard," Rosamund said.

He looked up then and smiled weakly. Relieved, perhaps. They were the first words she had spoken since he had entered the room, the first indication of her mood. But she was not angry with him, not any more, far from it.

"May I... explain about Marie?" His tone was hesitant, as if afraid she would explode again. But she no longer cared about Marie. Her rage seemed so long ago, as if she had been another person entirely then. Encouraged by her silence, perhaps, he went on, "Marie came here seven years ago, an émigré from France, escaping the troubles. She knew Madame Aubert, and Mother was looking for a new lady's maid at the time, so... Well, that lasted about three weeks. But Marie had a certain history that suggested... another role. It was Mother's idea that she should become my mistress. I was seventeen, and at that age... the idea appealed to me. But... I was never comfortable with the arrangement. Within a year or so it dwindled to nothing, and Marie found herself a new role. She runs this house now, which suits Mother. Ran it, I should say. I suppose we will need to engage a housekeeper, and Mother will get in a state again."

"I can run the house," Rosamund said. "If Lady Westerlea gives me her permission, I can certainly give orders on her behalf."

"You would do that?"

"It is what I have been doing for some time now at Woodside — since Mama died, and even before that. If it would relieve Lady Westerlea of worry..."

"That would be a kindness. Thank you. I suppose... we should have got rid of Marie years ago."

"One never likes to interfere in a smoothly running household," Rosamund said. "She was very good at that. I never had the least fault to find in her, whether as housekeeper or as maid. At least, not until she borrowed my clothes."

"That was very bad! Truly, it is so long since I ever thought of her as my mistress that I never even saw the impropriety in making her your maid. I dare not hope you will ever forgive my stupidity—"

"It is of no consequence," Rosamund said, and it was. Her head was filled with thoughts of that kiss, and there was no space left to be outraged about Marie.

"No? You are too generous, and I am undeserving of your forgiveness." He bowed his head momentarily. "Rosamund, we are supposed to dine at the Gellings' tonight—"

She gasped, hands to mouth. "Oh no! I had forgotten! What is the hour? I must change..."

"For myself, I cannot face company," he said, and there was a vulnerability in his face that she had never seen before. "I shall dine here. You may go or stay, as you prefer."

"Stay here? May I?"

He nodded. "Mother and Charity will go to the Gellings', and Aunt Faith and Mr Hathaway are both to dine out. It would be just the two of us... if you would like that. We could talk... I think we should talk."

She could not disagree with him, although what they were to say to each other she could not imagine.

~~~~~

It was the first time Rosamund had ever dined alone with her husband, and it was an oddly intimate occasion. They both wore full evening dress, since Robin and his mother always did so, and Rosamund had got into the habit of it. There was only one course, which was all Mrs Croaker could manage at such short notice, but there were eight dishes apart from the soup. Both parties were very subdued, and nothing was said that did not relate to the meal. Luckily, Mrs Croaker's skills had produced a buttered lobster, which Rosamund had never tasted before. Robin delighted in introducing her to new and sophisticated London delicacies, and so the discussion of the lobster carried them quite successfully through most of the meal, and only at the very end did they lapse back into silence.

This did not change when the servants withdrew. Rosamund picked at a dish of raisins and Robin rolled a walnut from one hand to the other, and the silence threatened to stretch over the whole evening. The situation was made worse by their proximity, seated together at one end of the large dining table. Rosamund struggled to think of topics for conversation, but every subject seemed difficult, and her whole body still thrummed from that kiss, turning her brain to blancmange.

It was Robin who broke the silence. "I do not know what to say to you," he said bleakly, his expression rent by sorrow. "Marriage... it is unexpectedly difficult. I worried about putting you into the right clothes, and whether you would know how to eat snails or dance the quadrille, all of which you can manage perfectly well. But I have no idea how to *talk* to you. Properly, I mean. About things that matter. And I do want to. I have a thousand thoughts in my head but they flutter about like birds and I cannot get them to settle."

It was such an accurate description of her own state of mind that Rosamund was taken by surprise, and could make no answer.

"We have been married for three months," he went on, "and I thought we were getting along famously. Now everything has changed. *I* have changed. I have no idea how to behave towards a wife."

"Nor I towards a husband," she said. "With Richard, he was already a friend…" She quailed a little, remembering her last savage encounter with him, and amended, "I had known him for a long time. But with you… we cannot talk about buttered lobster for the rest of our lives."

That brought a hint of a smile from him. "No, exactly. You asked once before if we could be friends, but I do not know how to begin."

The raw honesty of his words took her breath away. Impulsively she reached across the table to clasp his hand in hers. "I think you have never had the chance to learn about friendship. You would have made friends if you had ever gone away to school, or if you had lived amongst a mass of sisters and neighbours' children, as I have done. Robin, you have taught me so much about your life… will you allow me to teach you this? About the intimacy of friendship? Will you trust me enough?"

"I should like that." This time, the smile was broader and his expression lost a little of its anxiety. "How should we begin?"

"With honesty," she said. "When we are alone, you may talk to me about whatever you wish… whatever worries you. You may tell me everything you hope and fear." The terror written on his face told its own story. "Well, we shall work up to that, but there need be no restraint between us." He nodded but still looked panicked, so she said, "May I begin?" A relieved nod. "May I ask about Dr Hathaway? For I suspect he is closer to your mama than is quite proper for a married woman."

"He is... her lover, yes. Does that shock you? My father pretends not to know, but he tolerates the situation. My parents could not live together, you see. He never understood her needs and she was unhappy, so he allowed her to live in London. It is an unusual marriage, but they are contented with the arrangement." He hesitated, with a little frown. "Is this what friendship is? I thought..."

"It is a part of it... talking about whatever is on one's mind, freely and openly. And now it is your turn."

The panic was back. "I... have a great deal I want to say... about today... but..."

"I know," she said, squeezing his hand gently. "Your thoughts flutter like birds. Mine too. Today was... overwhelming."

His eyes widened. "*Yes!* And I do not understand it. It is too confusing for words."

"Then we shall wait until we are less confused," she said firmly, and was relieved to see his shoulders relax a little. "Talk to me about something else, then. Tell me what you were looking at through your microscope when I..." Her voice wavered, and his face filled with sudden understanding.

"I cannot remember," he said quickly. "I was too busy thinking about Ramsey."

"Lord Ramsey?" she said, surprised.

"Mmm. He came to me early this morning to ask permission to pay his addresses to Charity. I see you are as incredulous as I was, but I assure you he is quite serious. Did you have the least suspicion?"

"Not at all! He has been openly attentive, but I assumed he was flirting... either amusing himself with the most unlikely debutante or else piqued because she failed to display the proper degree of adulation towards the heir to a duke. Well, he will have his work cut out if he hopes to win her."

Robin was just about to raise his glass to his lips, but now he set it down again with a frown. "She will not refuse him, surely?"

"But she is not at all in love with him. She thinks him a rattle, or worse, and is not in the least impressed by his title. Not everyone harbours the ambition to be a duchess, or would be suited to the role. Although," she added reflexively, "Charity would make rather a good one, I think, if she could manage to avoid dropping her coronet or tripping over her ermine-edged gown at coronations."

He laughed, but said, tentatively, "You think, then, that love is the only proper foundation for marriage?"

"Not at all," she said gently. "I could hardly hold to such a view, given my own choices. But a woman must respect her husband, and Charity does not yet respect Lord Ramsey."

Robin stared at her. "But you were in love with Richard! You chose love there."

"With Richard? Oh, no. If I had been in love with him, I should never have refused him twice. Everyone assumed we would marry... neighbours, adjoining estates, how convenient! We were paired off in the entire county's mind almost from the moment of my birth. And I never had the least objection to the idea, for I liked him well enough. He was so gentlemanly, so very *eligible*. But there was no love on either side. He fell desperately in love many years ago, poor man, and I was very much his second choice."

"I have heard... something of Richard's case," he said. He opened his mouth as if to speak, then clamped it shut again, his eyes sliding away from hers. He was too well-bred to enquire, but she guessed the question that had almost been on his lips.

"As for myself," she said carefully, "there is no unrequited love in my past to complain of, indeed it has never been my fortune to experience either the pleasure or the pain of being head over ears in love. I came to my marriage untested in the ways of love."

"As did I," he said, turning his gaze full on her, and she felt that he understood her unspoken meaning very well. They had begun as strangers, and were now inching towards friendship. Perhaps one day that friendship would deepen to something more. Inside her, a spark of hope flickered into life.

12: The Road To Brinshire

Robin was relieved to have got through the evening without further mishap. Without losing control in that shameful way. The accusations he had hurled at her head, and then—! That moment of madness... and yet, she had kissed him back. How could she be so angry with him one moment, and then locked in a passionate embrace the next? How could he, for that matter? It was too confusing for words. And he still wanted to kiss her, that was the devil of it. Kiss her and more. How he longed for more! But he dared not, not yet, for what if she laughed at him, as Marie had, smirking and giggling in that irritating way she had? Rosamund would never smirk, she was far too ladylike, but he would know that she despised him, all the same. She would look at him in his nightgown and he would see the contempt in her eyes. No, he could not bear it. One day, he would have to force himself to do it but not yet.

So his thoughts ran as Brast fussed around, readying him for bed. Brast, at least, never thought him a contemptible specimen of humanity. Whatever attire he was arranging Robin in, Brast would end by stepping back and gazing at his master with a critical eye. "There, sir, you will do very well," he always said, and Robin would puff out his chest a little, reassured.

When Brast had tucked Robin into bed and drawn the curtains around him and finally departed, Robin lay still, not in the least ready for sleep. So much had happened that day — his whole life had changed. He and Rosamund had breakfasted as strangers and dined as... something else. For a short time that afternoon, they had unquestionably been lovers, but now he was less sure. Friends, perhaps. Yes, he rather thought they were friends.

The click of the door opening alerted him. Brast, perhaps? Had he forgotten something? But no, it was not the main door, it was the connecting door to Rosamund's room. Someone fumbled with the curtains, with an exclamation of annoyance as the opening eluded her. Rosamund! His heart hammered — what did it mean? What did she have in mind? The possibilities flew through his mind and he could not tell, even to himself, which of them he hoped for and which he feared, for it seemed to him that all options were fraught with danger.

The curtain whisked aside. "Ah, at last! Now, do not look so alarmed, I mean you no harm, only to talk for a little."

With the curtains out of the way, she set her candle down on a small table and clambered onto the far end of the bed. She wore only her nightgown, her hair hanging in a thick plait down her back. His breath caught in his throat at the sight of her.

"This is your first lesson in the intimacy of friendship," she went on. "Do you see my candle? See how small it is?

That is the Woodside rule. When we were little, my sisters and I would gather in one or other of our bedrooms before bed to talk over the events of the day without the constraining presence of the adults. As we grew, the practice became so ingrained and we talked for so long that Mama instituted a rule — we might only have an inch of candle burning. Once it sputtered, that was the time to stop talking and go to sleep. So you see, I have just an inch of candle and we may talk until it sputters. Or sooner, if we like. I shall not force you. But this is how we will become friends, by talking freely, which one cannot do in the dining room or drawing room, not in the same way. One is so much freer in a nightgown, do you not feel?"

"Freer?" he said, puzzled. "I always feel so… exposed in a nightgown. Defenceless. Like a snail without its shell."

She thought about that, her head tipped to one side. "Without a shell, yes. When I leave off my stays, it is very much like escaping from a shell. But exposed… I had not thought of it that way. Still, you are safely tucked up under the blankets, so you are quite safe."

That made him laugh. She was not in the least threatening, sitting there on his bed, chattering away as easily as at dinner — more easily, perhaps. He was not afraid of her, and when she prompted him to tell her something about himself that no one else knew, he remembered the time he had forgotten to pay his shot at an inn, only remembering days later. And he had decided that the inn had served a most indifferent meal, and did not deserve to be paid, so he had done nothing about it at first.

"Only I felt so abominably guilty about it that I sent them the money months later, under the seal of a letter."

"I have something far worse to tell you of," Rosamund said. "Once, the cook had made apricot tartlets for a special guest Papa had invited to dinner, who was particularly fond of such a dish. They were left on the windowsill to cool down, and I could not resist and stole one. Which would have been bad enough, except that I accidentally tipped the whole tray off the sill into the pigswill bucket so they were spoilt, and there were no more apricots to make more. The cook blamed the cat, and Papa shouted at the cook, and she took umbrage and gave notice, and then Mama was upset because she was a very good cook and now she would have to find another, and I never dared to confess. No one knows to this day that it was not the cat's fault at all, and we lost a good cook because of me. And the worst part of the whole," she added solemnly, "was that I was so horrified at what I had done that I threw away the one tartlet I had stolen, which was a shocking waste, because if there is one fruit in all the world I love above any other, it is apricots."

And by the time they had compared their favourite fruits, and told tales of secret orchard expeditions at certain seasons of the year, the candle had begun to gutter out and Rosamund had to run back to her room before they were plunged into darkness.

The next night she came again, and this time they talked of childhood memories. By the third night he was comfortable enough to sit up in bed facing her, and talk about Marie and how it had taken him a whole year to pluck up the courage to let her see him without his nightshirt, and then she had laughed and said he was just like a skinned rabbit.

"Well, that is very rude," Rosamund said indignantly. "A man's worth is not measured by the width of his shoulders or the muscles in his arms. Any common labourer may have a broad chest from working in the fields. A gentleman has a well-educated mind and perfect manners, and those qualities are of far greater importance than the strength of his arm. I am very glad she is gone, if that is how she spoke to you."

"I am glad of it too," he said, smiling at his lovely wife.

But then the candle guttered, and she slid off the bed and made her way to her own room. If only he dared to ask her to stay, to slip under the blankets and lie beside him, as a wife should. One day he would, but for now he dared not risk it. So long as he did not touch her, he was safe, he could maintain his control, could be a gentleman, even in a nightshirt and nightcap. But when he touched her... no, it was too great a risk.

Still, he began to feel he had a friend, now.

~~~~~

"You wished to see me?" Rosamund said. A summons to Robin's study was such an unusual event that she could not suppress a frisson of alarm. Surely they were getting on so well now that she had nothing to fear from such an encounter? Had she committed some unsuspected solecism? She could not think of anything.

But perhaps it was merely to do with Lord Ramsey, whose courtship of Charity had exploded into a crisis the instant that young lady had heard of it. Then there had been tears from her mother, glowering determination from Charity herself and bewilderment from Lord Ramsey, whose every attempt even to speak to Charity was soundly rebuffed. If they met socially, her faced closed up and she turned away from him without a word. He had been invited to dinner at Carloway House, and Charity had refused even to attend, eating from a tray in her room. It was distressing for everyone to watch so eligible a match thrown away.

Robin had a letter in his hands. "This is very strange," he said, waving it about. "My father writes that there has been some talk amongst the grooms about Richard's death, and now two constables from Brinchester are sniffing about, looking to unearth a crime. I am asked to go there and answer their questions. They seem to think I gained some benefit from Richard's death, but all I have gained, it seems to me, is the right to be dragged away from my home periodically so that my father may try to wrestle me into the mould of a country gentleman."

"No one who knows you could imagine that you wished for your brother's death," Rosamund said gently. "Must you go? You have obligations in town."

He sighed. "Father thinks I should, so that we may be rid of these people the sooner. I shall have to do it, I suppose. With luck, I shall not be gone above a sennight. You may ask Lady Carrbridge for assistance if you need a gentleman to escort you on any occasion. The marquess has brothers and cousins and uncles enough to fill a ballroom, after all. I daresay you will manage perfectly well without me."

His tone was not quite petulant, but there was just enough of the aggrieved in it to make Rosamund smile inwardly. "Should you like me to come with you?" she said.

His face lit up like a lamp. "Oh! Would you? You need not, if you had rather stay here and enjoy yourself."

"No, indeed, there is nothing to keep me here. Apart from the dancing, there is little that I would enjoy more than seeing the trees and fields and hills of home again. I have another idea — might we take Charity with us? She would have a little time away from Lord Ramsey and her mother's complaints to consider her future more carefully."

"That is an excellent idea. Perhaps she will even miss him, who knows?"

"Perhaps she will," Rosamund said, although she doubted it. But her absence would give everyone a respite from the drama, and might, if nothing else, give Lord Ramsey the opportunity to consider the wisdom of pursuing a lady who was absolutely determined not to have him.

And so it was agreed.

But that night, her boxes packed and her travelling clothes laid out ready for the morning, Rosamund brought out the broken rein and examined it again. It may be that she held in her hands the evidence that Richard was murdered. She could not — *would* not — believe that Robin had had anything to do with it, but perhaps some unknown person had murdered him for unknown reasons and remained unpunished. She knew what she had to do, yet she quailed at the prospect. It was too great a decision for her to make alone, but after some thought she settled on a solution. When they reached Brinshire, she would hand the broken rein to Lord Westerlea and he would decide what must be done.

~~~~~

Robin found the journey as tedious as any he had ever undertaken. The efficient Mr Simkins, his mother's secretary, had written ahead to secure accommodation for them. They followed his plan to the letter and so they found themselves greeted with deference and provided with comfortable rooms and excellent meals at their overnight stops. Nor were there any dramas on the roads, of broken wheels or sluggish horses.

The company, however, was not such as to raise his spirits. Charity, dragged unceremoniously away from her first season, was mulishly sulky. Brast, as always, made no overt complaint, but pulled a rug about his shoulders and maintained a martyred silence throughout. And Rosamund — ah, Rosamund! To the others, perhaps, she seemed just as normal, pointing out features of interest to Charity, or reading paragraphs from her guide book, but he knew her well enough now to detect the tension beneath her outward calm. Probably she saw the same in him, for occasionally she threw him a concerned glance. But there was no opportunity to be alone together or to talk privately, and since she shared a room with Charity, there were no cosy bedtime chats.

Holly Lodge had a chill air about it, despite the blazing fires. Its rooms had sat empty for months, and now exuded a neglected air, despite the number of servants there. Robin had not seen the house before, for when they had married there had only been one night before they were to depart for London, which they had spent at Westerlea Park. Now Robin looked around him with surprised pleasure, for the house was delightful, decorated and furnished with exquisite taste. He recognised a pair of paintings from the Park hanging in the drawing room.

"My father had a hand in this, I would wager," he said, amused.

"It is all his doing," Rosamund said. "He chose almost everything, and paid for most of it, I suspect. It is strange, but it looked rather outlandish to me before — very stylish, but not a comfortable house. Now that I am used to London ways, I see the beauty in it, and how the details that I thought so unnecessary act to enhance that beauty. These mirrors, for instance, seem to scream *'vanity!'*, yet they make the room so light, even though it faces north. And the wallpaper adds warmth."

He smiled, absurdly pleased with her perception. "Exactly. And the northern aspect is of no consequence, since the room will mostly be used after dark. You will receive callers in the morning room, I imagine, which faces east and south. Shall we go upstairs? You may show me the bedrooms before they become cluttered with our boxes."

Her steps were slow to ascend. From above, Charity's high voice could be heard chattering to the housekeeper, before her words were muffled by the closing of a door. Rosamund showed him his room first, which was rather a dull place, with dark wood-panelled walls and heavy, old-fashioned furniture. Richard's choice, no doubt. Still, Robin could redecorate easily enough, if he had to spend much time in Brinshire. His father had talked about the summer months, and how the weather would be more suitable for the two of them to drive around the estate and visit the tenants. Nothing further had been said about it, but he shuddered at the prospect.

"And your room?" he said politely.

Rosamund coloured a little, but very readily directed him to the adjacent room. There was no connecting door, but it was no more than half a dozen steps from one room to the other. Her room was quite different. The furnishings were light and pleasing, and he looked about him with approval.

"This is a pleasant room," he said.

"Yes," she said colourlessly, walking across to the window. But her gaze was not turned to the green lawns of the Park, but inwards, towards the large bed with its high pillows and neatly draped curtains, and her expression showed some deep emotion roiling within.

That was too important a matter to ignore, but he thought he understood her feelings. "Rosamund," he began. He was hesitant, but those midnight talks had given him the confidence to approach even so delicate a subject. "You must not be... anxious. You will have full control of the business. I will not be... demanding. There will have to be an heir sometime, of course, but—"

"Oh, no, no," she said, looking surprised. "That I understand. I am not anxious... about that. It is just that this is where Richard and I... where it happened."

"Where he seduced you?"

"Seduced!" She almost spat the word. "I would not have minded *that!*"

Shock and horror washed through him. "He *forced* you? Good God! My poor Rosamund!"

"It was not what I expected, you see," she said, hanging her head, her face ashen. "I had imagined it would be romantic and tender and loving... And afterwards, I was so ashamed. I did not hunt the next day, and I have always wondered... whether that contributed to his death. I promised him I would go... but I... I could not... and this room reminds me of that time."

She spun away from him towards the window, tears spilling down her cheeks. He crossed the room in three strides, and took her in his arms, holding her tight as sobs shuddered through her.

"Hush," he murmured into the silken top of her bonnet, hardly knowing what he said. "Hush now, my little one, hush, sweet Rosie, hush. There now, darling, it was not your fault." She trembled violently in his arms, and he himself shook with anger, thinking of what his brother had done to this beautiful, gentle creature.

There was a rap on the door, and they sprang apart, she with her face to the window, hiding her tears. It was two of the servants struggling with Rosamund's box.

"Mrs Dalton dislikes this room," Robin said, his voice harsher than usual. "Ask Mrs Greeves to prepare a different one."

Startled, they exchanged glances, then without a word manhandled the box out of the room again and shut the door.

"Thank you," she said, her voice subdued. She wiped her face with a handkerchief. "There — will I do?"

"You are a little pale, but then we have been travelling all day. Oh, Rosie..." Gently, he wrapped an arm around her waist and brushed her damp cheek with his fingers. "I am so sorry this happened to you. You need never be afraid of me, for I would never treat you so abominably."

She pulled away from him a little, and looked straight into his eyes. "I am not afraid of *you*, not in the least."

Her smile was so warm that he almost melted into incoherence. Her lips were enticing him and it was all he could do to keep himself from kissing her at once. More than anything in the world, he wanted to kiss her again, to be in that enchanted place of hot, sweet surrender, holding her, touching her, fired by the intensity of her response. But not yet. Control... he must be controlled for a little longer. Pulling her closer, he breathed, "Darling Rosie... I want so much to be the tender, loving husband you dreamt of, and to make you happy, as you deserve."

"Oh, Robin!" she whispered, and her breath tickled his cheek. "I want that too, so much."

It was exactly the answer he wanted. His voice was husky as he murmured into her ear, "Sweet Rosie... may I kiss you?"

"Oh, yes! Please!"

Instantly his lips were on hers, and she was pressed tight against him, kissing him back with a fervour to equal his own. Every time they broke apart briefly, gasping for breath, she murmured, "Robin! Oh, Robin!", over and over until they fell into the next kiss. If there had been a gale outside the house, it is doubtful whether they would have noticed.

There was no gale, only Charity, hammering on the door and then, when no one answered, bursting in so that they moved apart guiltily. "Oh, here you are," she said, eyeing them suspiciously. "Brast was looking for you, Cousin Robin."

"Brast can wait," Robin said loftily, although he was finding it difficult to catch his breath.

"Why, whatever are you doing? And why is your cravat askew, and Rosamund's bonnet hanging by its ribbons? Have you been *kissing?* Yuk!"

And Robin could only laugh, his arm firmly around Rosamund's waist.

13: Restraint

Rosamund could not stop smiling the next morning. Even with the cloud hanging over them both, her joy could not be dimmed. She smiled while she washed, she smiled while one of the housemaids fumbled interminably with her laces, she smiled as she braided and looped her hair around her head and she smiled as she arranged her lace cap. Then she skipped down the stairs, smiled widely at Mrs Greeves, to the housekeeper's astonishment, and smiled at the footman who poured her coffee in the dining room. And when Robin arrived, his eyes filled with affection, she smiled even more, heedless of the footman pretending not to notice.

"Good morning, Mrs Dalton," Robin said sedately. "I trust you slept well?" And then they both giggled.

But this happy state of affairs could not be sustained, for a note from the Park sat awaiting Robin beside his plate. "Father expects me at the Park at noon to meet the constables," he said, abruptly serious. "Ah, well. It is best to get it over with at the earliest opportunity."

"Certainly," she said evenly, although her insides were gripped with fear. "Once they have talked to you, they will go away." But their joy in the day was destroyed, and at the back of her mind was the thought of the broken rein. It sat quietly in her reticule, even while she drank her coffee and ate her bread and ham, and she knew that she still had the choice to say nothing. And yet... honesty compelled her to bring it forth.

"May I walk up to the house with you?" she said. "There is something I should like to say to your father in private."

He frowned, and she could see him wrestling with his curiosity. In the end, politeness won and he murmured only, "Of course."

It was both a convenience and a hindrance to be so close to the Park. One day, she was sure, she would be glad to be able to call upon Lord Westerlea and Miss Dalton so easily, but not today. Even dawdling and stopping to admire every vista and every unfurling rose, they could not make the walk last more than ten minutes.

Lord Westerlea was in his book room, grim-faced. Miss Dalton twisted a handkerchief in her hands, her cheeks wet with tears.

"Oh, Robin! Oh, Rosamund! How sorry I am that we should meet again under such circumstances," she cried weeping over each of them in turn.

"Come now, Aunt Mary," Robin said, cheerfully. "I am not on the gallows yet."

This brought forth such a bout of weeping that Lord Westerlea said testily, "Stop that nonsense, Mary! It will not come to that. But Robin, you had best leave off such frivolity, for these two men are determined to pin this crime on you."

"If there *was* a crime," Robin said. "Richard fell from his horse, as a thousand people do every year, and some of them die as a consequence. It is unfortunate, but it is hardly a crime. The coroner set it down to accident, and I cannot imagine how it might be otherwise."

"Nor I, but no one has yet been able to convince these men of the implausibility of it," Lord Westerlea said. "I have *some* influence over the authorities, I hope, but I have not been able to deter them on this matter. We must see it through, unfortunately. Rosamund, are you here to bear Mary company?"

"Rosamund wishes to speak with you privily," Robin put in.

Lord Westerlea's eyebrows lifted but he was far too well-bred to do more than bow in acquiescence. Robin and his aunt left the room, and Lord Westerlea waved Rosamund to a seat beside the fire. "Now, my dear, tell me what troubles you."

Haltingly, with many stumbles, she told him of Jed's arrival at Woodside with the horses and all the harness, and how she had noticed the broken rein and wondered at it.

"I do not even know why I kept it," she said, as she handed it over.

"Because you suspected a crime and felt it might be important," he said, examining it carefully. "It does look cleanly cut for about half its width. So then, at a critical moment, Richard would have applied sufficient force to break it. It still seems an unlikely way to kill a man to me."

"And to me," she said, calmer now that she had told her tale. "One could not be sure that the rider would fall, or, if he did, would injure himself. Richard was an expert rider, and knew how to fall off a horse."

"And do you believe that Robin did this?" Lord Westerlea's voice was neutral, but his eyes bored into her.

"Oh *no*, not for one second!" she said, shocked. "Robin is incapable of such an act, and besides, the last thing he wanted was to take his brother's place as heir."

Lord Westerlea gave a grunt of acknowledgement. "True enough. He likes his London life too well. And how do *you* like it, hmm? What do you think of the cream of society?"

"That there is kindness as well as selfishness amongst them, as in any group of people."

"And how does Robin measure? Is he kind or selfish?"

"Towards me, he has been kindness itself," she said, and could not suppress a warm smile from spreading across her features. "I am very fortunate in my husband."

"Ah," was all he said, but he smiled too. But then he looked down at the two parts of the rein in his hands, and the smile vanished. "It is my duty, I suppose, to show this to the constables." But he made it into a question.

"That is for you to decide," she said firmly, rising. "And now, I must return to Holly Lodge, for there is much to do today. Pray convey my apologies to Miss Dalton."

She walked the short distance home briskly. Home... how odd that sounded. For twenty two years that word had applied to Woodside, and for a few short weeks to Carloway House. Now she had to learn to live at Holly Lodge.

Her reverie lasted only as long as it took to reach the garden gate, for the sound of raised voices reached her even there. Before she had time to wonder what was happening and who could possibly be arguing in her house, a familiar curricle was led round to the stables, the horses still steaming.

Lord Ramsey.

He was on the doorstep, kneeling at Charity's feet, declaring in impassioned tones that he would love her for ever and could not bear to be without her and would be certain to pine away and die if she were so heartless as to reject him. She, just as passionately, declared that she would never marry him and would he please go away *at once* and importune her no further. Meanwhile, Mrs Greeves, the footman and a housemaid looked on in fascinated horror.

"Charity, pray stop squawking like a washer-woman and go to your room," Rosamund said briskly. "Lord Ramsey, do stop making a cake of yourself and come into the book room. Mrs Greeves, is there brandy in there?"

"Yes, madam."

"Excellent. Up you come," she said, hauling the marquess unceremoniously to his feet. "In here." With a snick, the door closed and blessed silence fell. She poured brandy, and held it out to him. "Here — drink. And do sit down. All this pacing about will not help."

"But I cannot bear it!" he cried. "Why will she not have me?"

"Sit, drink and stop being so melodramatic," she said. "Honestly, Lord Ramsey, you could have a promising career on the stage, but this is not the behaviour of a gentleman."

She would not normally have spoken so sharply to him, but Robin and the constables were at the forefront of her mind, and she had no patience to deal with his histrionics. Her brusqueness had its effect, however, for he sat meekly, accepted the brandy and drank it at a swallow. Silently she refilled his glass and set it down on a table at his elbow. Then she sat herself.

"Why will she not have me?" he said plaintively, calmer now. "I have money, position... everything most young ladies aspire to. And I keep telling her that I am quite reformed. My foolish wastrel days are quite over. But she will not listen."

"Lord Ramsey, how old are you?"

"I am eight and twenty."

"So you have been on the town for several years now, long enough for the season to be a commonplace to you. And do you know how old Charity is?"

"She is eighteen," he said stiffly, "which is a proper age for a woman to marry. She will enjoy a lifetime of seasons by my side, Mrs Dalton."

"True, but a season as the Marchioness of Ramsey is not the same as a season as Miss Charity Carrington. May I tell you a little of my own history, to explain it to you?" He nodded, and she went on, "You may be aware that, before my marriage to Mr Robin Dalton, I was betrothed to his brother, the late Mr Richard Dalton. Richard was the elder brother, the heir to the barony and estate, and I was the eldest daughter of the neighbouring estate. Our marriage was spoken of almost from the moment of my birth. It was expected, and we both understood that. If either of us had taken a different route, no one would have minded, but still, it was a much hoped-for match and I was perfectly amenable to the idea. I liked Richard very well, we rode and hunted together, we enjoyed each other's company, we always planned to marry. On my eighteenth birthday, he offered for me... and I turned him down."

He looked startled. "But why?"

"I had been out for a year by then. After all those years in the schoolroom, learning to be a demure young lady, constrained at every turn, finally I was free. For years, I was in my cocoon, waiting, waiting... until at last I could burst forth as a butterfly, and the whole world was mine."

She paused, struck by a vivid image of Robin's butterfly, stabbed with little pins that held it fast, so that it would never move again, all its beauty lost, all the life and colour and joy drained out of it. But she was not like that butterfly. She was pinned only by love, and that brought her more joy than she had ever experienced before. Robin had not pinned her, he had set her free.

Taking a deep breath to compose herself, she went on, "I went to balls and routs and picnics. I went on excursions to mountains and ruined castles. I dined out with every gentleman's family in this part of the county. And I *danced*... I love to dance, and every ball was a delight to me. I danced and was courted and complimented, men wrote poetry to me and brought me posies of sweet-smelling flowers, and I loved every moment of it. I had not a care in the world, no duties, no responsibilities, no demands other than the requirement to enjoy myself. Nothing could tempt me at that moment to surrender such sweet freedom for the constraints of a husband and children and a house. I was not ready for that. Richard asked me again the winter before last, but there was some talk then of a few weeks in London, and I so badly wanted to dance at Almack's, so I said no again. But it came to nothing, and last winter, I finally tired of it all. I had been out for five years, and at last I was ready to be a wife."

"Five years!" he said, appalled. "I cannot wait five years for Charity."

"Is she not worth waiting for?" Rosamund said gently.

"Of course, but..." He got up and paced across the floor. "Five years!" Then he sat again, and she was pleased to see that his expression was thoughtful, not dismayed. "I take your point. She is young, she is just now finding her wings and enjoying learning to fly. That is natural. I can wait, certainly, but there is no assurance that she will accept me in the end. She despises me utterly, and I have no idea how to convince her that I am a sober, respectable man now. She is all the world to me, and I cannot bear to face my life without her by my side. How may I win her, Mrs Dalton?"

"By being that sober, respectable man," she said. "Show her that you are worthy of her."

"Yes! Yes, I can do that." His face lit up with excitement. "If I compose a poem about—"

"No poems," Rosamund said firmly. "No courting, no special attention. She knows your feelings for her, so there is no need to repeat them. There is certainly no need to chase her halfway across England and hurl yourself at her feet. Take things slowly, but be always a gentleman. Restraint, Lord Ramsey, restraint."

"But if I am too restrained, she might fall in love with some other man, and then what would I do?"

"Why, you would wish her joy, and bear the disappointment as best you can, as a gentleman."

His face fell, and for a moment she was afraid he would break out into hysterics again. But he gave a twisted little smile and said, "I hope I am gentleman enough for that, and I do sincerely wish her happy, whoever she marries. And perhaps one day she will think better of me."

"And if she sees you less often for a while, that day may come the sooner."

"Ah," he said, with a sudden smile. "I understand you."

~~~~~

Robin returned to Holly Lodge about one hour later, accompanied by his father and the two constables, and Rosamund could see at once that matters were not going well. But Robin greeted her with a smile.

"Will you entertain Mr Williams and Mr Grout for a few minutes, Mrs Dalton? I need to fetch my microscope."

She was momentarily dumbfounded, but civility won the day. "Do please come into the book room. Ah, there you are, Mrs Greeves. Will you take some refreshments, gentlemen?

Some Madeira, perhaps, or sherry? Do sit down. Have you come from Brinchester?"

They sat, one round as a dumpling, perched awkwardly on the edge of his chair, with a nervous look on his face, the other long and thin, who lounged on a sofa quite at home and chatted with her in the easiest way imaginable. With a different accent and better tailoring, he could almost pass for a gentleman. Meanwhile, Lord Westerlea prowled about the room, refusing all food and drink, his face thunderous. Rosamund was deeply thankful that Lord Ramsey had left the house, for that would be a complication too many.

Robin returned carrying a large wooden box which he laid down carefully on his desk. "It will take me a little while to prepare the instrument," he said. "It has had to be disassembled for travel."

The thin man jumped up to examine the contents of the box, but evidently he was quickly satisfied and sat down again. Then, to Rosamund's dismay, he produced the broken rein from his pocket. "Do you recognise this, Mrs Dalton?"

Both Robin and his father turned at once to face him. "You will not interrogate my wife, Williams," Robin said coldly.

"All information is valuable, sir," Williams said blandly. "Our only objective is the truth. Truth and justice, that is our mission. Mrs Dalton was engaged to marry Mr Richard Dalton before his most unfortunate demise, and may have information of a private nature to impart. Perhaps it may be that there was a disagreement between them, and the lady thought better of the marriage."

"Then I should have cried off," Rosamund said coldly.

"Ah, but a fine lady like yourself wouldn't stomach the shame of being called a jilt," he said smugly. "It may be that you thought of a superior manner of releasing yourself from an unwanted betrothal, and you're a skilled rider yourself, by all accounts. You'd know all about what goes on a horse." He waved the rein about, smirking.

"Better to be called a jilt than a murderer," she said with icy contempt. "And if I were ever to contemplate murder, Mr Williams, I assure you I should choose a more certain method than hoping for a fatal fall on the hunting field. Poison is a much more sensible choice, I should have thought. Or a gun, for that is more likely to be fatal, and is readily set down to accident."

"Oh ho, you've thought this through, I see. Tell me more about this. I note that you haven't answered my question about a quarrel."

"I will not have my wife treated like a criminal to satisfy your prurience, Williams," Robin said in suppressed anger. "And if you mean to press charges against me, she cannot give evidence against me anyway."

"No, sir. That's very… convenient, isn't it?"

Robin looked ready to explode, but Rosamund put in quickly, "Do you truly have reason to believe that Richard was murdered, Mr Williams?"

"I do indeed, Madam, and this here piece of harness will prove it."

"What does it prove, except that the leather snapped?" Rosamund said impatiently. "The coroner was perfectly satisfied that it was an accident. Do you hunt, Mr Williams?"

"I, Madam? Oh no. It is too expensive a sport for such as I."

"But you have watched a hunt, perhaps? All country-dwellers see the hunt pass by from time to time."

He reddened slightly. "I... no, I've never seen it, no. Never lived in the country. I'm a townsman, myself."

"Then you can have no idea of the risks involved in following the hounds, Mr Williams. I have hunted for eight years now, and I never tire of it — the speed, the danger, not knowing what challenge might present itself next. It is an incomparable thrill, and the risk is part of that. One may fall at any moment, from uneven ground, or a mistimed jump, or a horse that startles for some reason. Every year, the hunt produces its crop of tragedies. Just this past winter Lady Delamore lost her life, also Sir Reginald Harbottle and a nephew of Lord Dryton. One does not need to look to murder to account for such deaths."

"And in how many such cases is it the heir to a title and fortune who dies, eh, Madam? And just when the younger brother has reappeared after many years. No, it's too suspicious by half, to my mind. We can't have younger brothers disposing of their elders, can we? The country would be in chaos. You make a good defence, Mrs Dalton, but it won't do. Your husband killed his elder brother and I'm determined to prove it." He chewed his lip thoughtfully. "Although maybe it wasn't him at all. Maybe it was *you* that did the murdering, Madam. Maybe you liked the look of the younger brother better the elder, eh? Same title, same fortune, and all you had to do was walk the short distance to the stables here and half cut through this here piece of harness. Hmm, now that I think about it, I like that version just as well."

And he laughed, a low, malicious rumble that chilled Rosamund's blood.

14: A Walk In The Woods

There was nothing to be said in the face of such obduracy. Robin silently assembled his microscope, his cheeks pale and his lips compressed to a thin line. As he worked, Lord Westerlea paced back and forth, back and forth, like a lion at the menagerie in the Tower of London. The fat constable ate cake surreptitiously and drank a large glass of Madeira. The thin one ate and drank nothing, watching Robin with a supercilious sneer on his face. Rosamund waited in an agony of suspense.

Eventually Robin was finished. "Will you pass me the piece of leather?" He slipped it beneath the microscope and peered through the eyepiece wordlessly for some time, twisting this knob and that.

"Well?" the thin man said impatiently.

"Come and see for yourself."

It was some time before the constable could see anything at all through the eyepiece, but at length he grunted and withdrew. Then his companion looked, and finally Lord Westerlea.

"It does not look like quite such a sharp edge now," Lord Westerlea said. "One may observe a raggedness suggestive of tearing."

Williams grunted again.

"There is one way we might learn more," Robin said. "If we make a cut elsewhere in the leather, just as Mr Williams supposes has occurred to the broken edge, we may observe whether that deliberate cut is the same as this edge or different."

The constable nodded his agreement, and Robin brought out his pocket knife and made a swift cut across the strip of leather, slicing it neatly into two. This he placed under the microscope, and examined.

"Ah," was all he said.

Reluctantly the thin constable looked too. His disappointment was written on his face. Lord Westerlea peered through the eyepiece, and exclaimed, "Why, it is quite cleanly cut! Not torn in the slightest. This is very different from the break that caused poor Richard's fall."

"Aye, so it is," Williams said.

"Then you are satisfied that there was no mischief here? That the rein was not cut?"

A long pause, then Williams said, with obvious reluctance, "I suppose it must be so. Still, it's very *convenient* that the heir met his end just then—"

"Enough!" Lord Westerlea said. "We have tolerated your insolence long enough. There is nothing about this broken rein which suggests murder. Looked at through the microscope, it is quite clear that the rein was *not* cut deliberately, not by my son, not by his wife, not by anyone. Do you agree?"

Williams said sullenly, "Aye, I suppose so."

"Then you agree that my son's death was no more than mischance, just another unhappy accident?"

A quick nod.

"Say the words, man, and let us be done with this nonsense."

"Aye. Mr Richard Dalton's death was an accident. But it did *look* like it was cut, my lord. We had to investigate, I'm sure you understand that."

"So you have investigated, and now you may leave us in peace," Lord Westerlea said firmly, holding the door open for them to leave.

When they had gone, Rosamund said quietly, "He is right about that, at least. Superficially, it certainly looked like a deliberate cut, even to me. That was why I kept it, after all. It is the greatest relief to know that it was not so."

Robin regarded her quizzically. "So all this time, you thought you were married to a murderer?"

"Oh, *no!* I never thought *you*— No, never that! But I did wonder how Richard came to fall, and the break in the rein looked so clean…"

"But not when viewed through the microscope," he said, with a smile that warmed her heart.

"Thank God for your little hobby, Robin," Lord Westerlea said. "I shall go and see what champagne I put in your cellar."

"Excellent idea," Robin said.

Rosamund heaved a sigh. She was still trembling with fear, but Robin saw her distress and understood, and at once sat down beside her and pulled her into his arms.

"There now, my sweet," Robin said. "It is over now."

"That *wicked* man wanted to see you hang! Or me!"

"I know, but that would never have happened. Even if the harness had been cut, no one could prove it was intentional or that either of us was in any way responsible for it. No judge would convict a man on such flimsy evidence. Or a woman," he added, with a little smile. "No one would imagine for one moment that you would kill a man to escape a betrothal. It is ridiculous, and Williams knew it. He was just trying to make us angry enough to let loose some useful information. I was his target from the start, but he never had any chance of success."

She shook her head, shuddering. "You cannot say what might have happened, and even if you did not hang, you would have been gone from me, and locked up in some evil prison. I cannot imagine how you would survive such humiliation, you who bathe twice daily and change your neckcloth four times."

He smiled then. "There are worse fates than to be without clean linen, my love. Not having you in my life — that would be infinitely worse."

He kissed her forehead, and then, very softly, her lips. Her arms went round him and she pulled him into a long, heartfelt kiss, so that they forgot entirely about the champagne.

~~~~~

For three days they were inundated with callers. Everyone of their acquaintance came to pay their wedding calls and to congratulate Robin on his escape from the clutches of over-enthusiastic law-enforcers. Rosamund managed to ride each morning before breakfast, but the rest of the day she sat in her drawing room with Robin, receiving so many visitors that they ran out of tea and had to borrow some from the Park. Lord Westerlea and Miss Dalton came every day, too, and Rosamund's father most days, and her sisters were constantly in and out of the house, thrilled to have their married sister home at last, and to admire her splendid new gowns and fashionable hairstyle. Rosamund had not realised how much she had changed until she heard her sisters exclaim over her stylish appearance.

Dinners were not quiet affairs, either, for Robin delighted in issuing invitations. One day it was Annabelle and Lucy, the next Margaret, Fanny and Papa, and then Lord Westerlea and Miss Dalton must be invited too.

Charity was subdued. Lord Ramsey had gone away without a word, and although she declared stoutly that she was glad that he was leaving her in peace for once, Rosamund thought the girl looked pale, and not her usual self.

"Well, I have had a long letter from Lord Ramsey," Robin said one day as they breakfasted, waving three closely-written sheets. "He apologises in very handsome terms for his behaviour, and informs me that he has gone back to Marshfields to rusticate for a while. He begs me to tell you, Charity, that you may return to town without fear of meeting him again this season." She looked at him, wide-eyed, but said nothing. "You may read the letter if you wish. I think you will find that he expresses himself very well, and feels just as he ought. He is quite ashamed of how he has pressed upon you, and promises to do so no more."

"Oh," she said in a small voice.

"Should you like to read his letter?" He held it out to her.

"I do not care what he has to say!" she declared, with a little of her former spirit, but she took the letter anyway, and disappeared to her room with it.

"Do you have plans for the day, Rosie?" Robin said when they were alone. "Shall we walk up to the Park? Father wishes to show me the accounts for the estate, and you could take tea with Aunt Mary."

"Later, perhaps," she said. "It is such a lovely, fresh morning that I am going out for a walk. If I go round by Claverley Lake I shall see if the swans have many cygnets this year."

"Claverley Lake? That is miles away!"

"Only four. I usually go round by the woods first, then past the lake and back across Woodside Farm. No more than ten miles altogether."

"Ten miles! Can William be spared for so long? Or one of the maids?"

She laughed. "I am perfectly well able to walk alone, Robin. I did so before I was married, and there can be not the least objection now."

"No, but... I do not like you to go so far without an escort. Shall you mind if I come with you?"

"Dearest, you would hate it." She glanced at his immaculate buckskins. "There will be mud, and it might very well rain later."

He smiled, and said with disarming simplicity, "I shall not mind a little mud if I am with you. Besides, you once said that an hour walking through the woods of Brinshire shows as many mysteries of the world as my microscope. I should very much like to see these mysteries."

They set off in cheerful spirits, as Rosamund pointed out every tree and flower and caterpillar of interest, and Robin stopped to examine such objects with his quizzing glass and collect a few small items in a glass jar. They crossed a couple of fields and he made no complaint when mud coated his top-boots and began to encroach on his buckskins. But by the time they reached the edge of the woods, he grew quiet and began to fall behind. Then it began to rain.

"Shall we turn back?" she said. "My cloak is keeping me very snug, but your breeches are getting very wet, and your coat will be ruined."

"It is not of the least consequence," he said brightly. "I would not for the world deprive you of your pleasure in the walk."

The woods gave some shelter, but when they emerged from its protective cover, Rosamund stopped, gazing out at the rain-washed landscape. It was not a downpour, but a steady, persistent drizzle that seeped through even the stoutest cloth. Robin sank onto a fallen log, his face a picture of dejection.

"Poor Robin!" Rosamund said affectionately. "You are soaked through."

"Do not be concerned. A little rain will not hurt me."

"Admit it," she said with a smile, stroking his face with one gloved finger. "You are hating this."

"Not at all," he said, but his face belied the words.

"There is no need to be polite with me, dearest. Be honest, now — you are wet, cold and miserable."

He smiled ruefully, with a little shrug. "I am certainly wet and cold, and I am beginning to be tired, but I am only a little bit miserable because I am with you, my darling, and that makes any discomfort bearable."

"Dear, sweet Robin! You pay me the most charming compliments." Pulling her cloak closer around her skirts, she seated herself beside him and rested her head on his damp shoulder. "But I would not have you made miserable at all, not even a little bit. You do not enjoy long, energetic country walks, so you need not take part in them, especially on rainy days. You would rather be looking at those caterpillars you collected in your jar." He laughed and acknowledged it. "Another time, we will choose a day without risk of rain, and we will drive out in your curricle to the far side of the woods, where the Frickham lane runs alongside. Then you may gather your caterpillars and I shall go for a brisk walk, and then we can drive home together."

"That sounds delightful, but you mistake me if you suppose I do not enjoy the rain. Long, energetic walks I confess hold little charm for me, except in the company they afford, but rain? I have the fondest memories of playing in the fountain at the Park when I was a boy, and standing beneath the gargoyles during a heavy rainstorm. It is only as I grew older and more fastidious about my garments that I have avoided rain. Let me show you how little I care about it now."

He jumped to his feet and pulled her up to stand beside him, the raindrops shimmering in his hair. With a bow, he hummed a few notes of a waltz tune. "Madam, may I have the honour of your hand for this dance?"

She giggled, but curtsied demurely. "Why, thank you, sir."

He hummed the tune, and they began to waltz, stepping cautiously. Rosamund's hood fell from her head and rain trickled down her face, but she did not care. She was with the man she loved, his arm securely around her waist, gazing into his eyes and nothing could prevent the bubbles of joy that rose inside her. They danced, they twirled, they hummed together, their steps not very accurate on the uneven ground, but it hardly mattered. Each time one of them stumbled or made a misstep, they both giggled but neither wanted to stop.

And then Rosamund stepped backwards, tripped over a fallen branch and went crashing down onto her back, with Robin half on top of her, both of them laughing so hard they could barely speak. So they kissed instead, and finding it satisfactory, they kissed again. It was a long, long time before they surfaced.

"Do you realise, my love, that we are lying in a puddle?" she said. "Your clothes will be ruined."

"Does it matter?" he said, gazing into her face with eyes alight with love. "They are not important. It is people who matter, Rosie, you have taught me that. I never knew how empty my life was until I met you. Have I told you how much I love you?"

"Once or twice. And I love you, too. I am the happiest woman alive."

"Even lying in a puddle?"

"So long as you are in the puddle with me."

"Likewise," he said, then added punctiliously, "although I am finding that this particular puddle, despite the agreeable company, is becoming rather uncomfortable."

"It is a particularly unpleasant puddle, now that you mention it," she said, smiling up at him. "So let us go home and take hot baths and put on clean clothes and be comfortable again."

"What a splendid idea."

They walked slowly back through the woods, arm in arm, muddied to the eyebrows, in perfect charity with the world.

~~~~~

Lord Westerlea insisted on holding a ball to celebrate the marriage of his son. It was arranged in great haste, since the principals were to return to London in a few days, but the baron would not wait until the end of the season.

"We will have another, more formal, affair then," he said, "but for now, I want to see my daughter-in-law dance."

"That is an admirable objective which I wholeheartedly support," Robin said with a smile, and Rosamund could only blush.

Somehow, in the few days available, the invitations were sent out, the musicians engaged, enough food and lanterns and flowers found. The hall and stairs and gallery were lit up as bright as the day, the guests arrived, the musicians played and Robin and Rosamund led the first dance. It was, for Rosamund, an evening as enjoyable as any she had experienced in London. She wore one of her London gowns, and her sapphires, and Robin had dressed her hair. She had not yet engaged a lady's maid, and the housemaids, while perfectly competent with buttons and laces, could not achieve a style that met Robin's standards.

As she looked around the room, she was beginning to understand just how much she had been transformed at Robin's hands in the few short months since her marriage. It was not that her Brinshire friends were dowds, but there was no doubt that they were a little old-fashioned to her eyes now. And they saw the difference in her, too.

"I love these little sleeves you wear, Mrs Dalton," said one matron. "Is that all the crack in town?"

"Such a delightful bandeau," said another. "I have never seen one like it before. And the trimming on your gown! How lovely you look tonight, Rosamund."

But it was the sapphires which were most admired, and even Lord Westerlea nodded approvingly. "Ah, so glad to see the dowry being put to good use," he murmured to Robin.

"Did you spend all my dowry on these jewels?" she said to Robin in a low voice.

"Not all of it," he said. "I would be hard put to it to spend twenty thousand pounds."

"Twenty—!" Rosamund had to put her hand over her mouth to stop herself speaking unbecomingly loud. "Impossible!" she hissed.

"No, I assure you. He pledged it long ago, should you marry Richard, and he made good on his word for me, too."

"Where on earth did Papa find so much money? I hope he has not impoverished himself, and has something left for my sisters. I had not the least idea he was worth so much. I always thought Mama's jewels would provide our dowries, but Papa could not find them. However did he find such a sum?"

"Well, he must have had it tucked away somewhere," Robin said easily. "And now *I* have it tucked away... all but the little bit around your neck."

They were interrupted by more arrivals, but even as she smiled and made her curtsies, Rosamund wondered how her father had managed to find so much money, and what he had had to do to obtain it. Something unpleasant, she supposed, for he was very much out of temper when the settlements were being drawn up. And now she remembered his odd reaction after Richard's death, when he had seemed almost pleased about it, doubtless because he no longer needed to pay a dowry. Except that she had promptly married Robin, and the dowry had been called for after all. Poor Papa.

He was at the ball, smiling genially, a glass in his hand, but she dared not ask him about it. He had always been non-committal on the subject of dowries. *'That is a man's business, child, so you need not trouble about it. There will be something for each of you, but only if I like your husbands, mind, so choose carefully.'* No, she could not ask Papa about it, and how could she worry about it for long when there was dancing to be had?

Charity danced every dance, and with every appearance of enjoyment, but Rosamund thought she was a little subdued.

"It is doing her good," Robin said to Rosamund, during a pause in the dance. "She will value him more if he is not so readily available, and in the autumn, perhaps we shall invite her back to town and perhaps they will meet again, what do you think?"

"Perhaps they will," she said, smiling. "We shall see. It does not do him any harm to be denied something he wants, and it does not do her any harm to be pursued by such an eligible man. Her reputation is established, and she may marry wherever she chooses, now."

For once, all of Rosamund's sisters were present. This was stretching good form, since Margaret and Fanny were not yet out, strictly speaking, but the nearness to their home and the position of their sister as the guest of honour established the appropriateness of their attendance. The two were permitted to dance only one set, and only with Robin, and the carriage would take them home directly after supper, but still, they were all at the same ball for the first time ever, and the sisters' excitement could not be contained.

Margaret and Fanny sat watching it all with shining eyes, too proud of their new ball gowns and too terrified of disgracing themselves to move. Rosamund could not stay with them herself, so they were left under the watchful eyes of Mrs Claremont and Mrs Sheridan. When each had their turn to dance with Robin, they executed the steps with expressions of intense concentration. Margaret, who was not a great talker at the best of times, answered his polite conversational openings monosyllabically. Fanny did rather better, and by the time they had gone all the way down the set was composed enough to talk more readily.

At supper, the sisters all sat together, while Robin willingly fetched punch for Rosamund, Annabelle and Lucy, and lemonade for Margaret and Fanny. Then he sat down between the two younger girls and listened cheerfully to Fanny's raptures about the evening, while Lucy, who never stopped talking, chattered over their heads about her own come-out and how exciting it had been.

"Do you remember that feeling?" Annabelle said to Rosamund. "Being almost sick with anticipation, and then finding oneself so tongue-tied, and having to mind one's steps all the time?"

"Everyone remembers their first ball," Rosamund said, with a laugh.

"The first and best," Annabelle said with a sigh. "No later ball quite compares. There are so many possibilities. One may look at every man and wonder if this will be the one to capture one's heart. Later, when one comes to know them better, one becomes disenchanted. Men can be so disappointing, sometimes."

"Not all men," Rosamund said, with a smile. "Sometimes, when one comes to know a man better, he is found to be not in the least disappointing." She caught Robin's eye across the table, and blushed at the affection so clearly visible there.

"Are you truly happy?" Annabelle whispered.

"Truly, I am."

"Ah. Then I am very happy for you, sister. I wished you joy on your wedding day, but it did not seem likely, then. Everything seemed so dismal, did not it? A year ago, we were all in pieces after hearing about poor Jeremy, and now look at us! Oh, look, there is Mr Cromwell, the man who almost—" She stopped abruptly, and coloured.

Rosamund laughed at her discomfiture. "The man who almost offered for me, you mean? I have no cause to repine over *that*. If he had offered... no, I am tolerably sure I should not have accepted him, but I confess I was a trifle piqued that I never had the chance to refuse him. Now, I heartily wish him well."

Lucy leaned across the table, and hissed, "That man over there, so splendidly dressed... is that—?"

"Mr Cromwell, yes," Rosamund murmured. "And I assure you, he is *not* splendidly dressed, not by London standards."

Fanny's eyes were round. "Is he what you call a... a fribble, Rosie?"

She tipped her head to one side, considering. "No, I should not describe him as a fribble. A coxcomb, perhaps."

"Or a popinjay?" Robin said, his eyes brimming with laughter.

"No, he needs even more clashing colours for that. You see, I know the difference, now, Mr Dalton. I can distinguish a coxcomb from a pink or a tulip or a fribble... and I have learnt to recognise and appreciate a beau."

"You refer, of course, to Mr Brummell," he said gravely.

With a laugh, she said, "He is a fine fellow indeed, but a little too plain for my taste. If he were here this evening, I would not regard him as the best dressed man in the room."

She left the words hanging in the air, but his eyes shone with pleasure.

After supper, the Winterton coach arrived to convey Margaret and Fanny home. Rosamund and Robin went out to bid them farewell, accompanied by Annabelle, Lucy and one of the Claremont boys, who had been silently following Fanny all evening with adoring eyes.

"Thank you so much for dancing with me, Mr Dalton," Fanny said in her soft voice. "I have had the most *wonderful* time." The Claremont boy sighed heavily at her words. "Goodbye, Thomas," Fanny said, waving shyly to him. He blushed puce and hung his head, making Fanny giggle as she stepped into the coach.

"And you, Miss Margaret?" Robin said as he handed her in. "Have you enjoyed yourself too?"

She nodded, quite overcome. "Thank you," she whispered, and he nodded an acknowledgement as he stepped back to allow the footman to fold away the steps and close the door.

"Drive on, coachman!" he called, and with a snick of the whip, the horses lumbered into motion.

Annabelle and Lucy, arm in arm, skipped back into the house, Lucy's chattering disappearing into the distance. Thomas Claremont, with another sigh, followed them with heavy tread, the footman in his wake.

"Well, Mrs Dalton, I hear the music beginning again. Should you like to dance the cotillion with me?"

"Let us not go back inside just yet. There is a little arbour just around the corner where we may sit quietly for a while, and, if you are very well-behaved, I may even permit you to kiss me."

"With such an inducement, I shall be sure to behave in a most exemplary manner."

He offered her his arm, and they walked slowly, their steps crunching on the gravel. The music of the dance drifted from the open windows above them, together with the low hum of conversation. It was not far to the small stone bench surrounded by roses.

"I do like being married," Rosamund said, with a sigh of satisfaction. "How pleasant it is to be quite alone with a gentleman without the least impropriety."

"Indeed," he said, "for I may put my arm around your waist without any fear of distressing you. And I may nuzzle your neck, like this..." She giggled, as he suited the action to the words. "Ah, your skin is so soft, Rosie. So soft, so sweet-smelling, so delicious... and your lips..."

There was a long pause after this, while Rosamund's lips were thoroughly kissed.

Eventually, he shifted slightly, so that he could gaze into her eyes without relinquishing his hold on her. "Dearest Rosie, we had such a difficult beginning, did we not? And my expectations of you were so faulty. I intended to mould you into my own image of a perfect wife. It took me far too long to realise that you were already perfect."

"No one is perfect," she murmured.

"You are perfect for me, and I adore you," he said, bestowing a delicate kiss on her nose. "My darling wife, I intend to make you very, very happy for our whole lives."

Rosamund had not the slightest objection to this delightful plan.

THE END

Thanks for reading!

I hope you have enjoyed reading this book! Now that Rosamund has found happiness, her four sisters would love to do the same. You can read their stories in the *Sisters of Woodside Mysteries*. Book 1 of the series is *The Governess*, featuring Annabelle, and you can read a sneak preview of Chapter 1 after the acknowledgements.

A note on historical accuracy: I have endeavoured to stay true to the spirit of Regency times, and have avoided taking too many liberties or imposing modern sensibilities on my characters. The book is not one of historical record, but I've tried to make it reasonably accurate. However, I'm not perfect! If you spot a historical error, I'd very much appreciate knowing about it so that I can correct it and learn from it. Thank you!

Find out more: If you'd like to know about my other Regency romance stories, contact me or sign up for my mailing list, my website is at http://marykingswood.co.uk/.

About the author

I write traditional Regency romances under the pen name Mary Kingswood, and epic fantasy as Pauline M Ross. I live in the beautiful Highlands of Scotland with my husband. I like chocolate, whisky, my Kindle, massed pipe bands, long leisurely lunches, chocolate, going places in my campervan, eating pizza in Italy, summer nights that never get dark, wood fires in winter, chocolate, the view from the study window looking out over the Moray Firth and the Black Isle to the mountains beyond. And chocolate. I dislike driving on motorways, cooking, shopping, hospitals.

Acknowledgements

Thanks go to:

Jane Austen and Georgette Heyer, who jointly inspired me to try my hand at writing a Regency romance.

Shayne Rutherford of Darkmoon Graphics for the cover design.

My beta readers: Lily Albiez, Shakera Blakney, Alicia Brazel, Mary Burnett, Quilting Danielle, Barbara Daniels Dena, Amy DeWitt, Melanie Savage, Keti Vezzu

Last, but definitely not least, my first reader: Amy Ross.

Sneak preview of The Governess: Chapter 1: The Will (January)

'To Mrs Price, Miss Winterton, Miss Margaret Winterton, Miss Frances Winterton. My greetings to you, and sincere condolences on the sad demise of your esteemed father. If convenient to you, I shall do myself the honour of waiting upon you at noon tomorrow for the purpose of conveying to you the material contents of the last will and testament of your late lamented parent. Yours in deepest sorrow, Horatio Plumphett of Plumphett, Plumphett, Witherspoon and Plumphett, Brinchester, Brinshire.'

~~~~~

JANUARY

Annabelle huddled in her favourite chair in the morning room, too numb even to cry. In the matching chair on the opposite side of the fireplace, Lucy sobbed noisily. Margaret had taken her usual place at the worktable, but for once her hands were still. She stared into space, white-faced and wide-eyed with shock. Beside her, tears poured silently down Fanny's face.

Annabelle could hardly take it in. Whatever was to become of them? Their ignominy could not long be concealed from the world. *'Have you heard about the Winterton sisters of Woodside?'* their acquaintance would say. *'Dreadful, quite dreadful.'* And indeed it was dreadful. She had no idea what they were to do.

Out in the hall, a murmur of voices as the solicitor was shown out. Poor Mr Plumphett! The reading of a will was always a doleful business, but he must seldom have had such bad news to impart. His usual urbane voice was high with distress. "I am so sorry, so very sorry," he had said, over and over. Perhaps he was still saying it, even as he was ushered out of the house and into his gig.

Doors opened and closed, the gig rattled away down the drive and in the hall, more murmured voices. Then Rosamund and Robin came into the room, their faces grave. At least Rosamund was safe, and that was a mercy. She had been wife these five years to Mr Robin Dalton, heir to Lord Westerlea of Westerlea Park, and could not be harmed by the scandal. One sister, at least, uninjured by the catastrophe.

But four sisters remained at Woodside, with no brother or husband to shelter them from the disaster.

"Lucy, do stop weeping," Rosamund said. "Tears never helped anything."

"But we are destitute!" Lucy cried. "Whatever are we to do! Thrown out of our own home! It is unbearable, and I will *not* go to the workhouse, I will *not!*"

"It will never come to that," Robin Dalton said firmly. "No one is throwing you out of Woodside. It is yours, after all, left to you all equally by your father, so you may stay here as long as you wish, until you have decided how to proceed."

"What option do we have?" Annabelle said. "The house must be sold to pay the debts Papa left. Then we shall be homeless and penniless."

"You will have a home with us for as long as you want," Robin said. "Penniless does not mean friendless."

Annabelle softened at once. She had not much liked Robin when Rosamund had first married him. He was something of a dandy, who spent more time before his pier glass than was proper for a man, and far too grand for country girl Rosamund. But Annabelle had warmed to him when she had seen how happy he made his wife, and how solicitous of her comfort. And now he would willingly take her sisters under his wing, too.

"You are all goodness, Robin," Annabelle said, "but we cannot possibly impose on you. You could not squeeze us into Holly Lodge, and we cannot inflict ourselves on Lord Westerlea. Nor would your mama want us in London."

"Then a small cottage in the village," he said. "With a couple of servants and your own good sense, you might live comfortably enough at very little expense."

"You have your own family to think of," Annabelle said.

"My wife's sisters are my family, too," he said mildly. "Besides, it is Rosamund's dowry which contributed to your father's ruinous financial state. We wondered greatly at the time where he had contrived to find twenty thousand pounds, but if I had known he had been obliged to mortgage the house to pay such a sum, I should never have agreed to it. Just because Mr Winterton promised it years ago, when he was better off, does not mean he was obliged to pay it when his circumstances had changed."

"And *why* did they change?" Lucy cried. "We were once very well off, and Papa bought Mama expensive jewellery every year for her birthday. Oh... is that ours, or part of the estate? Perhaps we will have something to live on after all."

She brightened visibly at the thought.

"No, all the good pieces have gone," Annabelle said. "Sold off or gambled away, who knows?"

"Not gambled away," Rosamund said thoughtfully. "Papa searched for them before I married Robin, and was very upset that they were missing, so it was not his doing."

"Perhaps Mama sold them to keep us afloat," Annabelle said. "Well, whatever happened to them, they are definitely gone, and there are only a few trinkets left. Would those be ours, Robin?"

"Mr Plumphett will need to advise on that point," Robin said. "He is also to let us have a full reckoning of all your father's assets and debts. His gaming debts were considerable, from what I have heard. I do not think we need to look further for an explanation of how the estate came to be so encumbered."

"If Jeremy had lived—" Annabelle began tentatively.

"It would have made no difference," Robin said quietly. "Your father's affair with the dice began many years ago, long before your poor brother lost his life."

"But what are we to *do?*" Fanny cried, with a sob.

"Nothing at all, yet," Robin said crisply, "except to dry your tears, Fanny, and Lucy, too, and wait for Mr Plumphett to report his findings to us. Then we may begin to consider how to move forward. And you must come for dinner again today."

"Yes, of course," Rosamund said.

"You have been so kind to us, sister, brother," Annabelle said. "However, I believe it would be best for us to return to our usual routine, at least for as long as we can. Who knows what the future may bring? So let us enjoy Woodside while we can."

Rosamund hugged each of her sisters in turn, and then she and Robin departed for the short walk to Holly Lodge.

"Well, if we are to dine here, I had better go and speak to Mrs Thompson," Annabelle said.

She found Havelock, the housekeeper, loitering in the passageway outside the kitchen.

"There now, Miss Annabelle, that's the worst over," she said.

If only that were true! Annabelle looked about her with new eyes, seeing, as if for the first time, the worn carpet, the faded paintwork, the chip taken out of the wooden panelling when the footman had dropped a whole tray of glasses. A footman... how many years was it since they had had a footman? Ten at least. The signs of increasing poverty had been clear for a long time, for those with eyes to see. But Annabelle had been beguiled by the comforting familiarity of her home. She loved its mellow stone, its odd wings of different ages and styles, its dusty, seldom-used corners and the passageways and stairs so well-known that she could find her way about blindfold. Her home.

She had been born at Woodside, they all had. Rosamund first, then Andrew who had died in infancy, then Annabelle, Lucy, Margaret and Fanny. Then poor Jeremy, sent away to sea at the age of twelve, to be made into a man worthy to inherit Woodside. But the sea had taken him from them on his first voyage, and there had been no more children after him, none that survived. Jeremy... the boy with the laughing eyes and the hair that always flopped across his forehead, no matter what he did to it. He would have been seventeen now, if he had lived. Almost a man. This mess would have been his responsibility, if he had lived.

This would never do! She must not get maudlin. What had happened had happened, and they must make the best of it.

"We shall be dining here today, Havelock," Annabelle said.

"Very good, Miss. Shall I give the orders to Mrs Thompson? You will not wish to be bothered with domestic matters today."

"Thank you, Havelock. She will know what to prepare. I cannot... cannot think about food at the moment."

"That's very natural, Miss, with the master only just buried and hearing the will, and all. But forgive me if I'm speaking out of turn, Miss, but... you look... I mean to say, it wasn't bad news, was it? The master didn't leave Woodside away from his own daughters?"

Annabelle gave a wry laugh. "Oh no, he did not do *that*. He left Woodside to us, equally, and he very generously left us all his debts, too. Tell me Havelock, have the servants been paid this quarter?"

The housekeeper shifted uncomfortably. "Well... no, Miss, not for a couple of years now, but it don't matter. Most of us have a bit put by, and we had a roof over our heads, and food on the table. We understood how it was."

Which was more than Annabelle had. No, that was not true. She had known perfectly well that there was less money than there had been, but she had assumed that Papa's income was being diverted to the gaming tables, leaving little for candles and coal. She had not suspected that the house was mortgaged. Rosamund had helped Papa with his accounts at one time, but whenever Annabelle had offered to do the same, he had bitten her head off, so she had never suspected the true state of affairs. They must have been living beyond their means for years.

She went back into the morning room. Lucy was alone there, still curled up in a miserable ball in the same chair. Annabelle took her usual seat on the other side of the fireplace.

"Where are Margaret and Fanny?"

"Probably in the attic, rearranging the furniture in the baby house."

Annabelle wished she had a comfort of that sort to turn to. Her books were her usual refuge, but today even that enticement held no charm for her.

"Fanny, at least, will be safe from poverty," Lucy said. "Mr Hawes will offer for her at last, and will whisk her away to Kellingborough. But as for the rest of us... you still pine for your lost love, I am a widow at two and twenty, and Margaret is too shy even to look at a man. I do not know what is to become of us," she ended tearfully.

"Now, do not start crying again, dearest," Annabelle said. "Rosamund is a little... *sharp*, sometimes, but she is quite right — crying never made anything better. As to what is to become of us, we have only three choices... to find a husband, to live on the charity of our relations or to find employment. The first two do not appeal to me, so I shall find myself a post as a governess."

Lucy swung round to plant her feet squarely on the floor. "No!" she cried, leaning forward in her anxiety. "You must not, Belle, truly you must not! The role of a governess is of all things the most disagreeable, neither family nor servant. I do not remember ours, but I know that the Claremonts' Miss Lackey ate all her meals in her room, like a leper. *Most* disagreeable."

Annabelle laughed. "That was because she was young and pretty and made sheep's eyes at John and Rupert... *and* at Mr Claremont, and so Mrs Claremont banished her, and she was too proud to eat with the servants. I should not be so proud, I assure you. No, it will suit me very well to be a governess, Lucy, so do not repine upon it."

~~~~~

For a fortnight, they continued almost as if nothing had happened. Callers came to offer their condolences, letter after letter arrived expressing sorrow to varying degrees, and the sisters sat in their morning room each day sewing handkerchiefs and trimming bonnets almost as if their lives had not come unceremoniously to an end. Only the quantity of black crepe reminded them. But several times Mr Plumphett's gig creaked up the drive, and once the handsome tilbury of Mr Martin from Martin's Bank in Brinchester, and each visit reduced Annabelle's spirits a little more. There was no money in the bank, no investments secure in the three percents, there were debts everywhere, some astoundingly large, and half the tenant farms had already been sold off. The remaining holdings were worth no more than two or three hundred pounds a year.

Something needed to be done. The sisters met in their father's book room, together with Robin and Rosamund, to discuss their plight.

"We cannot survive on so little money," Annabelle said, looking at the reckoning Robin had made of their financial situation. "It would be a reasonable income if we had no other obligations, but these debts... Do they all need to be paid?"

"Unfortunately, I fear so," Robin said. "If you were to sell the house and remaining estate holdings, you might just clear all obligations of that nature. It would only be possible to stay on here on such a low income if one of you were to marry a man of substance."

Annabelle tried not to look at Fanny, but she herself spoke up. "I do not have any expectations from Mr Hawes, if that is what you were thinking," she said, her chin rising defiantly. "He has not come near me since Papa died, and I must presume that any... any *regard* he might once have felt towards me has been extinguished." Tears sparkled on her lashes, but she held her head high.

"You are very brave, dearest," Annabelle said, and Margaret hugged her sister fiercely.

"I fear you may be correct," Rosamund said gently. "Lord Westerlea met Mr Hawes a few days ago at a card party. He felt Mr Hawes was avoiding him, rather, but when he approached him directly, Mr Hawes asked very politely after Robin and Aunt Mary, but made no mention at all of you."

"Which gives me a very poor opinion of him," Robin said sharply. "That is not the behaviour of a gentleman."

"Oh, but I cannot blame him for withdrawing," Fanny said, two spots of colour in her cheeks. "I daresay he cannot afford to marry without a dowry, and after all, there was no engagement between us. He had never spoken. I do not blame him in the least."

"So, your hero is proved to be no more than a mortal man, swayed by money like every other," Rosamund said impatiently. "Annabelle, Lucy, do you have any rich, lovelorn swains hidden away?"

Annabelle smiled, but shook her head.

"If I had ever been the type to attract rich, lovelorn swains," Lucy said, "I should never have taken poor Walter. Who marries a man of almost four score years except in desperation?" But she smiled as she spoke. "Dear Walter! Such a sweet man. I shall never find another like him."

"Then it seems that Woodside must be sold," Robin said sadly. "If you will give me the authority, I will engage to find an agent to manage the sale, and will myself undertake to settle with the tradesmen and pay the servants here."

"You are too good, Robin," Lucy said. "I do not know what we should have done without you." The others murmured their agreement.

"It is unfortunate that I do not have access to the income that will be mine one day," he said. "I could then have—"

Annabelle reached across to squeeze his arm. "Even if you had, it would not be prudent. The income to support us in such a house is gone. It must be sold and that is an end to it. So we must look to what we shall do next. We are agreed that we cannot impose ourselves on Robin and Rosamund. One sister might have been useful to them, but four is too great a burden. Elsewhere, we have few relatives close enough for us to apply for aid, and none at all on Papa's side, but Mama's family has been helpful. Aunt Letty and Aunt Pru can offer a home to one of us. Aunt Letty has recently suffered some ill-health and is almost bed-bound, and Aunt Pru writes that they would welcome a companion who could provide some company so that Aunt Pru is not tied to the sick room. They live very secluded, so perhaps that would suit Margaret. Do you think you could manage that, dear?"

Margaret nodded, but her face was pale.

"Mama's only brother, Uncle Arthur, writes that he has twelve children now, poor man, so his house is quite full up. However, his sister-in-law is unwell and in need of someone to chaperon her two step-daughters about. He suggests that Lucy might be acceptable — a respectable young widow and so forth."

"Oh, yes!" Lucy said. "I should love to, although... I am in mourning. Would it be quite seemly? To attend balls?"

"Your mourning period for your husband has passed," Rosamund said. "For Papa, there is no reason not to go about after the first month or so. You will not dance, of course, but you may certainly act as chaperon. Do you not agree, Robin? I have seen widows even in deep mourning at entertainments in London, although nothing of a frivolous nature."

"Oh, certainly," Robin said. "For a husband, it could not be thought of, but for your father it is not necessary to keep secluded."

Lucy smiled happily. "Then I should be very glad to do it."

"Excellent," Annabelle. "So that leaves Fanny and me."

"As it happens, I might have some possibilities for you," Robin said, with just a hint of smugness. "Aunt Mary wrote to her friend Lady Harriet Hay, do you remember her? Lord Carrbridge's sister. Lady Harriet supports a charitable endeavour for women with no family to support them. They make fashionable gowns for ladies of lesser means, those not handy enough with a needle to make their own. She employs a number of women as seamstresses, and would like someone of a more elevated background to talk to the customers."

"It sounds charming," Rosamund added. "The mamas bring their daughters to buy something special for an important ball, or to be married in."

"Oh, how romantic!" Fanny breathed.

"And you are so nimble with a needle, too," Rosamund said. "It would suit you admirably."

"Well, then," Annabelle said, with a sudden tremor. "It remains only for me to seek a post as a governess." After all the discussion and wondering and hoping and fearing, finally her family would be split asunder.

"Are you quite determined on such a course, sister?" Rosamund said. "I cannot bear to think of you in such a position. Governesses are hated by everyone — their employers, their charges, the servants. It will be miserable for you."

Annabelle was so tempted to answer with the stark truth. *I am miserable everywhere, so it hardly matters.* Instead, she said firmly, "My mind is made up, and I am well suited for the role, you must admit."

"Indeed, but… Well, no matter," Robin said. "If it does not work out, you may return to us and we will find room for you. For any of you, if you find your posts uncongenial. But if you are set on this, Annabelle, then there is a possibility. I asked Lady Carrbridge if she could help. Do you remember her? You will have met her in town."

"I remember her," Annabelle said. "I doubt she remembers me."

"Well, she meets a great many people, it is true. Here, read her letter."

She passed across a sheet of paper covered in neat script. After the usual salutations, Annabelle read, *'There is an old friend of Lord Carrbridge's who might be in need of a governess. His wife died last year, leaving him with three young daughters to raise. The poor man is distraught and hardly knows what he is about, so he has not yet thought what he should do for them. Lord C has written to enquire of him if he would like a recommendation for a governess, but we have not yet heard from him. I will let you know if we hear word from him. In the meantime, do tell me a little more about your sister, so that I may know how best to describe her accomplishments. Constance Carrbridge.'*

"This came just today," Robin said, holding out another sheet.

'So happy to tell you that Allan would be delighted to offer Miss W a post as governess. It had been on his mind that he should do something about the matter, but had not the least idea how to go about it. If she is all that you say, I am sure she will do very well there. His mother is in residence, so there will be not the least impropriety. He lives at Charslby, near Kenford in Cheshire, and is a very pleasant, amiable man. All the Skeltons are charming. I know his sisters quite well, and they are delightful. I am sure Miss W will be very happy there. Constance Carrbridge.'

Happy. Annabelle could not imagine being happy ever again, but she was content to be unhappy at Charlsby. Robin wrote to accept Mr Skelton's offer, and to Charlsby she was to go to begin her life as a governess.

END OF SNEAK PREVIEW OF *The Governess*

Made in the USA
Monee, IL
20 July 2022

10048864R00132